I0544784

JADE MARSHALL AND RAVEN HUSH

EVERNIGHT PUBLISHING ®

www.evernightpublishing.com

Copyright© 2025

Jade Marshall and Raven Hush

ISBN: 978-0-3695-1202-4

Cover Artist: Jay Aheer

Editor: Lisa Petrocelli

ALL RIGHTS RESERVED

WARNING: The unauthorized reproduction or distribution of this copyrighted work is illegal. No part of this book may be used or reproduced electronically or in print without written permission, except in the case of brief quotations embodied in reviews.

This is a work of fiction. All names, characters, and places are fictitious. Any resemblance to actual events, locales, organizations, or persons, living or dead, is entirely coincidental.

JADE MARSHALL AND RAVEN HUSH

DEDICATION

To the wild souls who dare to love in the shadows,
who crave the thrill of danger and passion,
and who find solace in the arms of the unearthly.
May you always find strength in the darkness
and love in places you least expect.
For those who believe in the impossible,
this story is for you.

JADE MARSHALL AND RAVEN HUSH

SINNER'S END

Forgotten Shadow Lords, 1

Jade Marshall and Raven Hush

Copyright © 2025

Author's Note

Sinner's End may contain triggers for some and includes dark themes. As readers, we find trigger warnings to be spoilers, but as authors, we understand that they are sometimes necessary. Although we are not going to list each one, there are many, please feel free to check either of our websites for your specific trigger(s). There is significant sword crossing within the male members of the harem. If this is not your party, you are forewarned. Please do read the list for your safety.

Jade Marshall: www.jademarshallauthor.com

Raven Hush: www.sofiaaves.com/raven-hush-paranormal-romance

For those of you who wish to go in blind, please remember that this is a work of fiction, and we DO NOT condone or wish to romanticize any of the situations or actions of the characters. Please read safely.

Happy nightmares.
Jade & Raven

Track List

I Hate Everything About You - Three Days Grace
Sweet but Psycho - Ava Max
Radioactive - Imagine Dragons
The Pretender - Foo Fighters
Shipping up to Boston - Dropkick Murphys
Bleed it Out - Linkin Park
Walk - Pantera
Freak on a Leash - Korn
Skinny Little Missy - Nickelback
Halfway to Hell - Jelly Roll
Jack - HARDY
Hard to Love - Lee Brice
Bloodstream - Ed Sheeran
Don't Let Me Down - Fame on Fire and Arcaeus
Can You See Me In The Dark? - I Prevail & Halestorm
I Will Follow You Into The Dark - Death Cab For Cutie
Just The Way You Are - Pierce The Veil
F**k You - Sleeping With Sirens
Some Nights - Like Moths To Flames
I Knew You Were Truble - We Came As Romans
Royals - Youth In Revolt
Stitches - State Champs
Heathens - Twenty One Pilots
Close - Chainsmokers ft Halsey
Bark At The Moon - Ozzy Osbourne

JADE MARSHALL AND RAVEN HUSH

Prologue

Ever wonder what it would be like to wake up with no memory of who you are, or what you did the day before? To forget everything and start with a clean slate. No past crimes, no embarrassing moments, or memories of broken hearts. Ruined friendships, family. No ... nothing. A blank page waiting to be written.

Only, how do you start a story when there's no baseline? What are the benchmarks you set yourself against, if you can't remember your last failures, or how far you fell? If it hurt when you landed. What makes you fear rejection, or how to succeed in business, in relationships?

All the questions that come from one simple line. A wish unthought out for its basic complexity.

To be reborn.

Alone.

Why would a person—any person—want that? What did they do that was so horrific they desired most of all to forget everything they'd ever done?

Every*one*.

Maybe I wished that once, and wondered what it would be like. But I guess I'll never know.

Or maybe I do.

JADE MARSHALL AND RAVEN HUSH

Chapter One

A Change is Coming

Adreana

Have you ever had the feeling of being alone even when you're surrounded by people? Being utterly and completely alone even when you're among your closest family and friends? For years I felt that way even when I was in a crowd. But the last year has been different. I haven't had a moment where I felt alone once.

Because of my watcher.

"Did you hear a word I just said?" Emma, my twin sister, asks, shoving at my shoulder.

"No," I reply, continuing to scan the park we are walking through.

My American pit bull terrier, Daisy, comes speeding my way with a ridiculous smile plastered across her face. The steel-blue monster tackles me to the ground, slathering me with kisses until I struggle to breathe before she speeds off again.

She loves coming to the park as much as I do. I rescued her from the pound the moment I stepped out of high school and we haven't been apart since. She is the only thing I love unquestioningly and without forethought. For three years, Daisy has been my only companion, the reason I still have a remaining sliver of sanity. She helped me to not feel so alone in a world full of people.

Daisy and my watcher.

I feel watched and followed every minute of every day. I can't explain where this feeling is coming from but

I know I should have a different reaction to the situation. I shouldn't feel safe or cherished. What I *should* be feeling is fear. I know that, but it doesn't change a damn thing.

"I want you to come with me to the Halloween party at Harken tonight," my sister says again, finally drawing my attention.

"Are you nuts? I hate that place," I reply with a frown. "Everyone is on something, and that fucking man is always lurking."

I can't fucking stand Mana. The man is too attractive for his own damn good and he knows it. I've only been there a handful of times, but I always manage to run into him. Most of those times are because of something my stupid sister did.

"Please. You can't let me go alone," Emma says softly, casting her eyes toward the grass beneath our feet.

I inhale deeply through my nose before exhaling. I know this ploy. She is trying to manipulate me but that doesn't work anymore. It's another thing that has changed since I started to be watched. I went from a wallflower, terrified of my own shadow, to someone who has a backbone and speaks her mind.

"Don't do that." I nod as I scan the area for Daisy. "Your crocodile tears and fake sadness don't work on me anymore, Em."

"What happened to you?" she sneers, clearly irritated, her false tears forgotten. The difference between her actual personality and the fake one she uses is as stark as night and day. "What happened to my sister?"

"You mean, when did I stop following you around like a lost puppy? When did I remember I had a mind of my own?"

"You know that isn't what I meant." Emma faces me with a frown, her hands firmly planted on her hips.

"You may not have said it but it doesn't make it any less true. Our entire lives, you led and I followed. You spoke and I agreed, even when I was sure you were wrong. That's what really bothers you."

"What the hell, Addi?" she gasps her shock. "You've never talked this way before."

"I didn't, but these have always been my thoughts and feelings. And now it's time for things to change," I say, clipping Daisy's leash in place before walking away. "I'm not just going to blindly follow you anymore, Emma."

"Where are you going?" she yells behind me.

"Away!"

I hear her continue to talk but I steadfastly ignore her. For as long as I can remember, I have always danced to her tune, done whatever she wanted. She has always been the more outspoken, free-spirited twin, but now it's time for me to start living my own life.

Don't get me wrong, I love my sister with my whole heart. She is the only family I have left but I can't stand her. I never could. But then, you don't have to like someone to love them.

Yes, I am fully aware that I won't allow my only living family member to walk into the damn den of iniquity by herself. Yes, I will end up joining her at Harken tonight. But you can be damn sure I will make my displeasure known every step of the way.

A tingle spreads down my spine, and awareness flows through my veins. My watcher is back. Breathing deeply, I try to remain calm even with the adrenaline spike coursing through my veins. I want to stop and seek my watcher out, but I don't. I never do.

The fear of them leaving holds me back. Do they know I am aware? Or will that scare them off? I don't want to lose this feeling. Also, I am terrified of ending the mystique that surrounds my watcher. I honestly don't know if I want to find out, even if the curiosity is killing me.

I can't explain the way I feel which is why I haven't said a word about it to anyone. Being watched like this isn't something creepy or scary. No, it feels like I am being protected, even though I don't have an idea why I would need that sort of attention. Or deserve it.

So instead of doing anything, I continue as if nothing is out of place.

"How do you feel about some ice cream, girl?"

Daisy gives me a lopsided smile and a little yelp. She starts walking faster, pulling me along, and I laugh at her enthusiasm. People may say animals don't know what we're talking about but as my beautiful rescue leads me toward the ice cream parlor, I know they are full of shit.

"Hello, Adreana!" Mr West smiles brightly as the bell above the door rings. "And the beautiful Miss Daisy." He reaches down and scratches my pup affectionately behind her ear.

"Hey, Mr West. How are you feeling today?"

"You know, same old, same old." He chuckles as he scoops out some of the sugar-free peanut butter and banana ice cream he makes special for all the dogs in the area.

Growing up just outside of Portland, Oregon, you would think I was just one of many faces. But the community is very close-knit in the suburb we grew up. You know the kind of community you see on TV and think could never be real. That's where I grew up. Everyone knows each other and is always in each other's business. Even with the city just being out of reach, we almost have a small-town feel.

It's irritating in a way I can't explain, but also beautiful. When my parents died in our last year of high school, the entire community banded around us, watched over us, and helped us. I will never be able to repay what this community, this town did for me. And I would never be able to put into words just how grateful I am.

I stay here for that reason. Hoping one day I will be able to pay forward the kindness that was shown to me and my sister.

The other side of the small-town feel is always having people in my business. I couldn't fart without the whole town knowing and having an opinion about it. But I have learned to take the good with the bad.

"Are you headed home?" Mr. West asks as he hands over the ice cream, glancing out the window. "It looks like a storm might be rolling in."

"Yeah, just stopped for a treat." I smile and hand over some cash.

With a wave, I walk out of the parlor and head to the house I have lived in my entire life, and now share with my sister. It's nothing special, hell, it's not even a pretty house, but it's ours.

All the way home, the feeling of being watched and protected never leaves me.

I wouldn't have it any other way.

****

My dreams are vivid. Hands, lips, and skin. Dark hair, light hair, tattoos, bulging muscles... I'm not sure when they started, but I know I have them every night now. Scratch that, every time I sleep. Even if it's only an afternoon nap. I always wake up hot and bothered, the feel of several hands still burning on my skin.

Perhaps if I had someone in my life, someone to slake my lust and take care of my needs, it wouldn't be so bad. But I'm alone, and I've only had mediocre sex a handful of times with the same guy. I don't even see any prospects on the horizon.

I don't have any interest in any of the men in town, and I certainly don't see myself with any of my sisters' friends or one of the drug-addled idiots that frequent Harken.

So, I did the next best thing a girl can do and ordered myself a battery-operated boyfriend online. The sleek black box arrived yesterday. After waking from my afternoon nap and a dream that has me begging to be fucked, I seek out my new purchase. Opening it up I stare at the intimidating silver phallic form nestled in its bed of purple velvet.

Desperate times call for desperate measures.

Slipping fresh batteries inside, I lie back down on my bed and fiddle with the speed and intensity settings before pressing it against my sex through my panties. *Holy shit.* The vibrations roll through my already sensitized body. Outside, thunder rolls through the clouds as heavy rain pelts against my bedroom window. I never close the drapes anymore, hoping to give my watcher an unobstructed view.

Awareness rocks me, and the feeling of being watched is more intense than ever before. The gaze caressing my heated skin from a distance serves to make this experience more erotic and even a little taboo. I mean, who the fuck masturbates for their stalker's viewing pleasure?

Pulling my panties aside, I allow the object in my hand to slip through my folds and nudge at my entrance. My orgasm is already cresting, the dream I woke from earlier still riding me as I twist the dial to the highest intensity.

A scream rips from my throat as my orgasm washes over me. I hope my watcher sees everything. I want to entice them to approach me. I need to know if my watcher and one of the strangers in my dreams are the same person.

I want...

JADE MARSHALL AND RAVEN HUSH

Chapter Two

Welcome to Hell on Earth

Mana

Blood tinged with a hint of sin drips from the end of the needle jammed into my skin. Even with tape wrapped around the puncture mark, my darkness ekes out, staining my flesh with the taint of my kind. Demon kind, waltzing amongst humans like I'm the same and expect them not to notice the increasing differences between us.

"One of these things is not like the other things." I hum the little ditty in my twisted way, watching my man potter about at my side in the unused asylum's frigid, underground room. The perfect place to create a drug the previous inhabitants would have given a fragment of their souls to possess.

Alonzo sees the change in my demeanor as he drains me, I'm certain of it. But I pay him well enough, and that's what keeps him in line. His loyalty remains with the highest bidder, and none other. No one else can give the twisted Chemist what I do.

A good thing my father allows me unlimited power over some aspects of my life. That boon creates a comfortable hiatus for my study of the overworld to better understand how to endlessly torment and torture their kind.

At least, that's how I pitched my little holiday venture.

I'm so full of shit.

An hour in sunlight is worth an eternity in any

dark realm, and I've bartered myself a full mortal life of the stuff. Shit, I nearly giggled hysterically as I backed away from *his* throne built of ash and souls.

For the next sixty or so years I'll exist in a reduced, aging body until my bargain expires. I fully intend to enjoy every second of my rule over men before I return to my place at the hellkeeper's side. Sunshine, hot pussy that's not actually burning from the inside out when I pierce their flesh, and lollipops.

That last part might have been misconstrued. The gift I was given turned out to be a mortal curse that has left me, at the human age of thirty, a pincushion prisoner for a drug of my own making in an underground criminal empire on which I maintain a tenuous grip.

Sometimes, I wonder why I left hell at all.

"Another gallon to go, *my lord*." Alonzo smirks, flicking the needle with a dirt-encrusted, ragged nail rather than the vein.

Pain ricochets along my arm, and I discover extra nerve endings I forgot I possessed in this form.

"I appreciate your candor." I grit my teeth, watching the man's scarred, pale fingers worm their way along my flesh. "One day, I'll repay you in kind."

And sear the flesh from your brittle bones, one layer at a time.

I believe humans have seven layers of skin. I'll enjoy exposing every single nerve ending of his to my blackened flame while I fuck his ass with a cock that spews acid the color of my blood. A gift I could request and know the promise will be held for a not-too-soon future for both of us.

Cooking sinners from the inside out is fun. I get to experience all their suffering that way. Here, I am a lot more harmless. No acid in my veins, though my taint remains. Same for my cock. I haven't cooked anyone for thirty years and … it's nice. Relatively speaking.

Alonzo fusses with his vials, swirling their contents and studying the color. He checks a cheery little timer on the scarred wooden table at my side while he sucks on his teeth. A disgusting habit. I'll enjoy removing his gums sometime.

"It's paler today."

I blink at him. "I beg your pardon?"

"The stain that ForgetMeKnot flourishes on. It's … fading. Like you're becoming more like the rest of us." He speaks baldly in an honest exchange of information as we've always done, though omissions are permitted.

Human. Mortal.

I never said anything, and he hasn't asked. But it's hard to hide that my blood isn't the claret hue of the rest of his race. Not that he'll oust me. There's no reason for him to screw his cash cow into the ground before I've run my course in benefiting him.

Plus, he won't find a payday greater than my drug.

I sigh. "You want to test it again, don't you?"

"I won't fuck with our distribution." He shrugs, rolling heavyset shoulders and cracks his neck. "Or I can take double." Alonzo taps the little timer and twists the dial.

A groan rips from my throat and I manage to conceal the wince that follows. Fuck me, being human is more of a pain in the ass than advertised. Maybe sunlight isn't worth it after all.

But it is.

I nod slowly, collecting my thoughts as my mortality drains from my veins. I've never stopped to see how much it takes for this body to bleed out, but I can't die. I was aware enough to add that clause into my bargain. I might be a flaccid meat bag for a short period, but I can't cross over until my penance is due. Which means that no matter what happens to me, I am stuck living in this realm for the next sixty years.

It seemed so simple a deal but the look in *his* eyes told me I should have been more cautious of signing away the only real life I would ever be likely to claim before I returned to my eternity of servitude. Freedom wasn't real. Everything was a facade. Fake, fake, motherfucking fake.

"Fine. I suppose you have a subject in mind?"

Alonzo's thin mouth covered in sparse, unmanicured hairs splits in a truly horrific grin, and that's before he breathes. "I've got just the man. Actually, he reminds me of you."

"There's no one like me." I inhale carefully as he backs up, fixing me with an unsettling stare.

"Well, not quite like you. More like what you're not." He laughs, the high-pitched sound unbecoming his endless girth in a duplicitous, psychotic sound that echoes around the cavernous room.

"I see." I relax, but my heart, that traitorous organ I cannot control, thrashes wildly in my chest. Sweat gathers beneath my hairline and trickles along my spine in an itchy, unreachable path.

Who said being human was a joy? Lying fuckers.

Alonzo has guessed at more than I expected. I will have to be more careful. If he realizes he can overpower me, turn me into a pump for the forgetfulness drug, I'll be more of a prisoner than I already am. That deal really sucks from this point of view. Then his words register.

"What do you mean, like me?"

Alonzo backs off, slipping a dirty knife from his belt and trailing it along the stone walls that remind me forcibly of home. "He's like you, just ... bats for the other team."

The door to the old asylum's shock room closes with me its only inhabitant, locked to a chair the twisted mind of a human designed for the devious pleasure of watching others suffer.

Beside me the little timer ticks the seconds of my mortality away and I count the pints of my sins collected in tiny vials.

****

My arm throbs beneath the little plaster decorated with tiny pink daisies. Alonzo swears it's the only box he could find, and I plan some extra playtime for him in the afterlife. Not that he gives a shit, the man can't think further than his next payday, and his expenses eat through his stipend well before the next rolls around.

I stride through the double doors toward my office, the only plushly appointed room in this godforsaken place where the sun rarely shines.

That's the other part of my bargain. To live in a place not of my choosing. While I imagined a sandy paradise for my travels, what I earned myself was nine decades in a mostly sunless city. Portland, Oregon, was where I landed. It looked all right, hell, I can even see the water from the top of the abandoned building beneath the almost constant cloud cover.

I just can't get to it.

My limits end at the edge of the asylum's grounds and spread as far as that cloud cover allows on the other side of the city, terminating at a house that borders an old graveyard, its turrets overlooking the hallowed ground.

Sinner's End.

It's not even abandoned. A pair of not-so-innocent sisters lives there, and my drug has started to worm its way into their social lives. Ekeing away at their fears and replacing their petty concerns of social canceling into a recklessness that drives them directly into my path. One girl is just like the rest of her tribe—vapid, thoughtless, concerned only with herself. The other is … different. Not that I care for a child barely out of her swaddling rags, even when her moans roll through the quiet grounds while her dead rest in their earthen graves.

My father's sense of humor carries into the overworld, and I don't care for it a fucking inch.

And so, I turn my attention to the parts of my life I can control. *I'm becoming more like them every day.* Too damn much. Soon I'll be chasing skirt and breeding a blonde human woman, for fuck's sake.

"Who is our hamster today?" I flick the handles on the panneled, polished doors, soaking in the cold air let into the space by the open windows opposite my hardwood desk.

If I can't have a sunny beach and fake tits in my face, I'll damn well experience a cold, fresh breeze sharp enough to freeze the clit off a sorority slut. My brand of torture differs from my kind, as does my peculiar humor, or so I've been told.

"Reporting for hamster duty, sir." A tall Arayan looking man towers over me. Crystal pale eyes the color of pristine snow stare at me from within a chiseled, tanned face. This asshole clearly gets plenty of sunlight, and I instantly hate the fucker.

"Jesus Christ." I look up at him, unused to feeling short on this plane. At over six feet tall—not under—that doesn't happen very often. "I thought hamsters were tiny."

"Maybe you can dissect me for the purpose," he suggests softly without a single frisson of fear.

I watch him with the sort of care one eyes prey

they aren't sure won't turn about and latch onto them with rabies-infected fangs. "Perhaps we can. Seat."

"I thought it was *sit*." He arranges himself in a perfectly still "L" shape on the hard wooden chair designed to make the average person uncomfortable. He looks right at home.

"So they do." I wait, expecting him to try to fill the silence, but he stays as still as before. It's fucking unnerving, and I suspect the tanned asshole isn't even trying. I sit opposite him in a leather gamer chair that fits my ass to perfection. "Do you have a name?"

He mumbles something under his breath, but before I can call him out on the shitty habit, he fixes his gaze over my shoulder. "Lethe."

"Lethe." I turn the name over in my head. "Got a first name, Mister Lethe?"

"No."

"Last name?" I raise my eyebrows, my patience redlining.

"Just Lethe." His gaze never wavers, and he never looks directly at me.

If this isn't the strangest conversation I've had in this place, then I don't know what is.

"All right, Just Lethe. Why do you want to try my drug? It's powerful, and you won't remember anything afterward. What is it you're trying to forget?" I watch his eyes as they oh-so-fucking slowly slide to meet mine.

"I've already forgotten," he says simply.

Pain is etched behind those crystaline, inhuman eyes that sees everything, a curse in itself, but he doesn't know why.

I do, and Alonzo was right. Lethe is like me, and he does indeed bat for the other team. Well, he *did*.

Because fuck my life if I haven't found myself a fallen angel who doesn't even know he is one.

JADE MARSHALL AND RAVEN HUSH

Chapter Three

Fuck My Life

Adreana

Don't you dare fucking judge me!

Yes, I am outside Harken, dressed more like my sister than myself. Even though I want to protest and lie, saying I don't know how I ended up here, I can't. As per her usual methods, my sister has manipulated me into doing something and being somewhere I never would have chosen on my own.

I can honestly say this is the last straw. She has dragged me from my home out to an abandoned asylum on the wrong side of the tracks, literally.

Standing outside the imposing building, I stare up at the disheveled red brick facade.

Harken.

To Listen.

What kind of name is that? Why the hell would I want to go inside? The Gothic building looks like it may crumble at the slightest gust of wind. I can't think that I want to hear anything a single soul there has to say.

Emma grabs my hand and tugs me past the ridiculously long line of people waiting to gain entrance. "We don't wait in line!"

She is giddy at the idea of getting in before everyone else with her A-list card. It makes her feel special, the preferential treatment. I would rather wait outside in the cold night air freezing my underdressed ass off, hoping to never gain entrance.

"Emma," the burly bouncer greets with a toothy

smile. "Who's your little friend?"

I have never seen the same staff twice. They could be rotating their places and I just miss it every time but my guess would be that the staff turnover here is high. I know I wouldn't be able to work here for any extended amount of time.

My sister giggles in a pitch so high it makes me want to rip my ears from my head. When did she become this irritating creature beside me? When did I start to dislike her this much? I miss the days when we were joined at the hip, doing everything together and sharing all our secrets. Now, I spend as little time with her as possible.

"She's my sister." Her eyelashes flutter as she gazes up at the bouncer. "How does it look inside?"

"Same old, same old," he says and chuckles. "Dancing, drinking, all the fun things we know we shouldn't be doing but can't live without."

Emma bounces up and down in her sparkly, powder pink minidress, her boobs nearly popping out the top. The bouncer has his leery gaze glued to her cleavage, and I want to gag.

"Why don't you ladies head inside?" he mumbles, pushing the door open. "Have fun."

The moment my heels hit the tiles I know this is a bad idea. I swear the walls whisper secrets at me. My skin is crawling at the thought of staying here a moment longer. A deep base reverberates through me, seducing me. There are people everywhere, bumping and grinding on the dance floor beneath strobe lights. I watch as men and women shimmy up against one another, hands touching, lips tasting. It's beautiful chaos.

Some are dressed casually, while others are dressed for Halloween. Cats, vampires, and what looks lie a mummy mingle with the other patrons.

"What are you staring at?" Emma shouts in my ear.

I shake my head before focusing my attention back on her. "I need a drink."

"That bar," she yells with a broad smile, pointing in the direction she means before stepping away from me.

"Emma," I say harshly, pulling her back by her wrist. "Don't disappear on me tonight."

"Don't be a baby," she jests and I want to slap some sense into her. "You're a big girl. Now, let's party!"

With her hands thrown above her head, I watch her shimmy between the writhing mass of bodies on the dance floor as she makes her way to the bar.

Skirting around the dancers, I make my way to one of the two bars situated in each of the back corners of the room. It is a lot more opulent inside and I keep finding new details to marvel at.

Mana keeps the inside of the place immaculate, unlike the outside, and every time I step foot in here it seems he has updated or changed something. The bar itself is sturdy, made of dark cherry wood, and polished to gleam and reflect the strobe lights. The barstools are covered in black leather with high backs and I am more thankful than words can express to find one available.

I rarely wear heels or dresses, both of which my sister has coerced me into tonight. She tried to get me into a canary yellow minidress but I was able to work my way into something more my style. Black. I tug the dress down my thighs as I take the last available seat and wait to be served.

The man behind the bar is tall and muscular, though not bulky, with wavy blonde hair. Dressed in black pants with a deep purple button-up shirt and black tie, he seems a little out of place. His sleeves are rolled up to exposed muscular forearms covered in colorful ink.

I definitely haven't seen him before.

The man gives me a sexy grin as he approaches and my heart does a little flip before I realize Emma is right beside me. Of course he wasn't admiring me the way I was him. How stupid can I be? A man like that is much better suited to someone like my sister. The pretty one. The one all the men look at while they overlook me.

"Kaleb," she purrs seductively but he doesn't even spare her a glance as he stops in front of me.

"I haven't seen you here before." His voice is deep and smooth. "What can I get you to drink, gorgeous?"

"Just a beer. In the bottle," I say, shoving my shock aside.

He nods before turning to my sister. "Your usual?"

She nods before turning to glare at me as he moves away to get our order. "What the hell, Addi? I've been trying to get into Kaleb's pants for months!"

I return her glare as my beer is placed on the counter. I don't respond to her asinine accusations. It's not like I was trying to get his attention. Besides, he is a bartender. It's his job to flirt.

A man whistles from the other end of the bar and Kaleb waves him off as he leans across the bar top, slate gray eyes focused fully on me.

"Tell me your name."

Emma huffs loudly before grabbing her fruity blue-and-green cocktail and leaving me alone at the bar. So much for spending time together. The moment she didn't get her way she deserted me. I knew she would disappear on me. Same shit, different day.

"Addi," I say, not giving any forethought to telling this stranger anything about myself.

Another whistle sounds from down the bar and Kaleb glares in that direction. I watch a man twice his size pale underneath his gaze before holding his hands up. Interesting.

"You should see to your customers."

"I am seeing to the most important one right now." He winks. "The rest of these chuckleheads can wait." He smirks and I wonder if this line of flirting gets him laid often.

"Won't your boss be mad?" I ask, sipping my beer from the bottle.

A thought crosses my mind. What will it take to ruffle Mana's perfect facade? To make him crack and lose that perfect control he is so famous for? Will his staff being less than considerate of all the patrons be enough? Not that it matters.

"My boss is very ... open-minded." He seems to be laughing at an inside joke. "But enough talk about things that aren't you. What brings you to Harken tonight? I've never seen you here before."

"How can you be sure? There are probably thousands of people that make their way here every week."

"I can assure you I would remember."

He continues to flirt. It's a great feeling, to be desired. Occasionally his gaze dips to my cleavage before returning to my face and I know this is more than simple, friendly banter. He really is interested.

"My sister has a thing for you," I mention with a smile. "So you can stop flirting with me."

"Sister?"

"Emma."

Throwing his head back he laughs freely. "Sorry to be the one to break the news to you, but your sister has a reputation." At my confused frown, he continues.

"She's a slut. And I would rather chop my dick off than stick it in what is probably the most worn-out pussy in Oregon."

Beer goes flying from my lips, and uncontrollable laughter bursts from me. My sister has always been promiscuous but I never expected to hear it put that way.

"Sorry," I mumble, cleaning my chin with the napkin he offers me. "I've never heard it stated quite like that. But I can assure you it isn't news."

Looking up at Kaleb, I find him staring at my tits before licking his lips. Beer has dribbled down into the valley between my breasts, clearly drawing his attention.

"I need to clean up," I say standing from my seat. "Which way is the bathroom?"

"The red door over there." Kaleb points.

I glance in that direction, two doors clear to see. Red and blue, side by side. Making my way around the writhing mass of bodies on the dance floor once more, the usual awareness works its way down my spine and I know my watcher is near. Did he follow me? What does he think of how I am dressed? Will he finally come to me tonight?

I quickly head inside the bathroom, wanting to hurry. If I'm lucky, tonight could be the night I finally come face to face with my watcher. Protector? Excitement sweeps through me at the mere thought. Grabbing a few sheets of tissue paper from the dispenser, I lower the straps on my dress and start cleaning myself up.

"Such a pretty little treat." The words are breathed into my ear before I find myself shoved against the wall, face-first.

Chapter Four

For Her … Anything

Lethe

I can feel the desire rippling through the insurgent's body a moment before I tear him from hers, slamming the back of his head into the brickwork behind me, and dropping his unmoving form to the floor. Is he dead? I tip my head to one side. *Do I care?*

As I stare at the stunning girl in the skintight black dress, I decide I don't. Mana won't, either, from the way I watched him rip a man to pieces with strength no human should possess.

I know my talents are wrong, just as his are. Perhaps we're alike, him and me, and that's why I am drawn to this place with its torture and echoing screams I can still faintly hear when the music stops and silence holds. The sounds are etched into the very stones of this house of literal horrors. It's obscene that underage teens and a few legal and tempting pieces like the one before me party here. A disgrace, really.

A single tear trails her cheek, and my groin tightens in the black leather pants Mana insisted I wear as part of my staff costume.

Not that I've seen anyone else dressed like a fucking gimp. All that's missing is the helmet. My chest is encased in a tight leather vest with boning that tightens around my waist, and there are cut out holes for my nipples. Maybe I'm the disgrace, not her.

This should be a place of reverence where the souls trapped in the thick walls and the hard-packed dirt beneath our feet have a hope of freedom. We should pray for their eternal existence before we become another of their legion.

A whimper escapes her throat, while mine dries. My first night on the fucking job and here I am, lusting after a girl who must be at least half this body's age, ripping men off her. It won't be the last, I am certain of it. Not with the grateful way she watches me like I'm some golden boy, some heroic savior.

Not like the identical sister who trailed her fingers over my nipples on her way to the bar earlier. The little slut stank of overuse. I half expected her to drop to her knees in the middle of the dance floor.

Moss green eyes stare at me unwaveringly. Even though I just killed a man before her—he's not moving and darkness slinks from his body as if trying to make its final escape—she isn't running or screaming.

No, this girl is different, and some innate part of me recognizes she's mine to protect. Not that I remember anything of my past life, so that last could be utter bullshit. It probably is.

"I see you've started the night well already." Mana leans against the end of the hallway, his bulk blocking out most of the light. His gaze fixes on me and I know he hates that I'm taller than him, my rigid stature I can't seem to rid myself of more imposing than his. "Shall I call for a clean-up crew?"

"I got it."

"Fuck me." The bartender I met earlier in the night during the pre-party staff meeting—Kaleb—barrels past Mana without so much as a *by your leave*, and the boss man doesn't acknowledge him. "Already? We're gonna have a talk." Kaleb fixes me with a hard, unyielding stare, and I see why Mana keeps him.

"He was assaulting the lady, got a little handsy. I

pulled him off." I shrug, but the motion turns into a twitch, and I roll my shoulder painfully to still the unconscious urge.

If I can't control my past, I'll fucking well tie knots around every damn hour of my future.

"Perhaps a little less force next time," Kaleb murmurs. "Boss likes to torture assholes like this. You've ruined his playtime." His gaze slides sideways. "Hello again, sweetheart. Addi, was it?" The man's demeanor changes subtly. He rests one hand on his belt, sliding his thumb across the tooled leather.

The girl watches the digit's progress, her lips parted just enough to make a sweet "O" shape, the perfect place for a man to shove his—

"Pheromones. Clean it up," Mana barks, jerking us all out of our reverie.

The girl jumps, quickly righting her dress. Shit, we *all* do, and I drop to my knees.

"I said I got it." I heave the body over my shoulder, ignoring the still-dripping blood warming the backs of my thighs, and stride away.

"Thank you," the girl whispers.

At this distance I shouldn't be able to hear her, but I do. I glance back over my shoulder to where Kaleb leans one arm over her head, his dipped to whisper in her ear. His fingers brush across a darkened patch at her shoulder, inked fingers lingering on her skin.

Smarmy bastard.

Green eyes watch me, not him, as I carry my burden away from her. But those eyes don't stay locked on me forever. The moment she turns away, pain rips through me, a searing pressure that builds outward.

I force myself to face forward, almost running along the never fucking ending corridor, and burst through the doors at the other end, but the empty hallway doesn't offer the freedom I crave. My fingers burn, every nerve ending screaming. I know what's coming.

Corridor after corridor I run in an eternal nightmare, the screams of those long-departed heralding my wake at one who will soon join them.

I must get outside.

I sprint the last dozen paces, bursting shoulder first through a locked door, and ignoring the bruise that will doubtless form there tomorrow. If I don't get away from the building, something much worse will consume those within.

Maybe it will free the souls.

Maybe new ones will be added to their number.

I make it as far as a small hillock beyond the main building, the crisp night air assailing my searing skin. That fluctuation in temperature is all my body needs before it does the only thing I know, the first thing I remember. I hunker down, the asshole's body still draped across my shoulders, weighing on the back of my neck, but the pressure doesn't last long.

Not now.

The pain intensifies, like hellfire or something so much worse violating every cell in my body. My world goes white, then—

Nothing.

A weightlessness, floating above everything, or below. Up is down, and down is…

I slam face-first into the ground. My hands smoke before my eyes, and those eyes water with the returned sense of mortality that clearly isn't mine. Ash drips from my shoulders. I hope the man was dead before I exploded, or whatever the fuck just happened. Not a pretty way to go, otherwise.

That's twice it's happened, now. I have no idea what set off my first round. But killing clearly lit the ember within me this time. Or maybe it was the spike of protective lust I experienced at helping the girl. Maybe I could do something else wrong today, and make it a hat trick.

"What a pretty display."

I can fucking well *feel* Mana's smirk.

Swallowing, I straighten and dust the ashed man's cinders from my shoulders. "I'll clean up and be right back."

"You'll work exactly as you are." Mana's eyes narrow in the darkness where he loiters in a doorway, not a single toe over the threshold like he can't bear to tread the ground outside Harken Asylum.

I growl, the sound ripping at my still searing teeth as my body cools. Our eyes lock in a battle of twisted wills, though neither of us manage to be the victor in our combined, merging anger.

And while we fight it out in silence, the sister—a poor facade of my obsession—emerges from the building beside Mana, dressed in a pink piece of candy floss and looking far less edible. Her chirpy voice screws with my zen, or maybe my anger where it filters into the night over the souls trapped within Mana's home.

"Oooh, fireworks!"

She claps her hands and squeals like a child. Finally, Mana looks down and takes her hand in his, drawing her back into the bowels of the impromptu club no doubt to pump her full of alcohol and drugs and other bodily fluids.

I dust the remaining ash from my exposed nipples and follow them, the taste of a ruined soul bitter on the back of my tongue.

That won't wash out anytime soon.

The door to the asylum slams at my back, locking me in with the other tortured souls.

****

"What a fucked-up night." I lean into the cold water that won't wash off the taint of the man who threatened the girl no matter what I do. How hard I scrub, how hot the water.

I resort to turning it as cold as it will go in the hope of dousing the ember still lit somewhere so deep inside me that I wouldn't be able to find the wretched thing, even if I let Mana carve me open and dig through my flesh with his bare fingers.

"For a first night, it wasn't bad. You killed someone and disposed of the body neatly, from what I heard. Made a lot of people happy, I'm sure." Kaleb steps under the spray beside me in the cavernous, communal showers the asylum afforded its prior occupants.

How many souls were tortured here? How many inmates were physically assaulted? I swallow back bile, the acid rupturing my throat until iron coats my tongue.

Good. Anything is fucking better than ash.

"Toughen up, princess." A hand—an unwelcome one—slaps my ass.

Kaleb gives me a hard sideways look and walks away, leaving his shower running.

I flick his faucet off. *Thanks for the support, my man.* But not paying attention to the asshole at my back is my mistake, if only for a moment.

His body slams mine into the cold tiles, courtesy of the icy water I've been drowning myself in for half an hour.

"Fuck off," I grouse, placing my hands on the tiles. The faintest hint of bleach lifts to my nostrils, burning my nose hairs.

My ember ignites, and I close my eyes, already

wary. *We've been here before tonight.* I have no idea what will happen if I explode inside a building, and I doubt Mana wants to find out, either. That he was witness to my uncontrollable shame darkens the room for a moment. My vision flickers, or maybe the lights do.

"Such a pretty boy. Maybe you should kneel for Mommy," my assaulter's voice hisses in my ear. Alonzo, Alonsi? I can't remember the asshole's name. They're running together.

One hand reaches around me to grip my cock hard. An unwelcome and disgusting touch. I grit my teeth, willing my control back before I swallow ash again. Once a night is enough for me.

"Hands off, you withering penile stain," I murmur. Breath flows in, and my ember settles.

I smile against the bleached tiles. *Now we get to play.*

Alonzo's cock presses to my ass, his balls giving mine a love tap. I have no idea if I'm into men, but this sort of approach does nothing for me. The vision of the girl with green eyes flitters through my mind, and I know one thing above all else. *I want her.* To touch her, bathe her, protect her. Love her.

Another thing out of my control, but this time I find I don't mind.

"Did you say you want my cock to rip your pretty asshole apart?" he hisses into my ear. For a single, frozen moment I know just how the girl felt tonight with that man on her.

Addi.

I step out of Alonzo's hold like he weighs nothing, his presence stripped away as I twist his wrist and slam him face-first into the wall right where I stood a second before. "Is this how you play with your food, you pathetic excuse for a man? Is it fun?"

I slide a searing finger along his spine. Fine fissures of smoke and the scent of burning flesh sears the oxygen between us in their wake. My burning finger, the only part of me I let heat to the point I scar him with every touch, rests over his hairy asshole. My heart is joyous as I press forward, pushing my poker-hot finger into his puckered hole.

"Stop!" he screams, his body convulsing against mine. "No! The fuck!" His hands claw, scrabbling at the slicked tiles, and the scent of bleach joins melting flesh.

I press harder, and the ring of muscle pops around my finger. His screams intensify and before I can kill the man, burning him from the inside out, I withdraw and wash my hands fastidiously beneath the showerhead with an excessive amount of soap. I hate getting shit beneath my nails.

Flicking off the faucet, I step over Alonzo's whimpering body where he lies on the white tile and stare at Kaleb who watches me with curious but not frightened eyes. Perhaps I fit into this place better than I expected.

"Some of that bleach would come in handy." I grab a towel and rub myself dry.

"I'll mention it to the cleaners. Should I make sure I don't drop the soap near you, homie?" Kaleb flicks my ass with his towel.

A bold move, considering what he just saw.

"Only if you intend to damage me the way that fuckwit did to the girl. Addi?" I frown. "Is there more to her name?"

"Addi is the only bit I know. Cute as fuck, and not as much a slut as her sister." Kaleb rolls his neck and something pops. "That one will fuck anything."

"Who's the slut?" I throw my towel over the door of the locker I was assigned. Three. I trace the curly digit engraved into the flaking metal door, adding a few extra loops to the pattern, though I don't understand why.

There are so many parts of myself I don't recognize, parts that expose themselves every day. Like the explosions or the burning finger. Shit. Someone should write a comic book.

"*Her.*" Kaleb's muted whisper draws my attention to a girl on her knees at the far end of the showers that, in my haze of death and ash, I failed to notice.

Her mouth is wrapped around—tries to wrap around—a cock that would be better suited to a horse than our boss. She's still dressed in that hideous pink confection I saw her in at the door with Mana after my ... disgrace. But while his face is watchful as he gazes dominatingly down at her, not a hint of pleasure flickers across his visage, and hers is...

Blank. In its entirety. Like who she is ceases to exist. He presses his cock deeper and her throat bulges in a disgusting display of power. Neither look like they want the pleasure the act should bring them, in this casual encounter of body parts, over the bliss one gifts their partner for the pure joy of knowing that other person enjoys their touch.

One more thing I've learned about myself today: I can be a fighter *and* a lover.

The green-eyed girl, the pink fluffy one's sister, flickers through my mind. There is a female I could lavish attention on. Then I recall the loathing look Mana bestowed upon her, the way Kaleb leaned over her body, claiming her. How she reacted to him.

Didn't she? I run the encounter through my head, but it's not clear in any version I replay if she wanted the bartender's attention or not.

Mana finishes in an unnerving silence, creamy liquid tinted green pouring from the girl's mouth. He drags his cock away and she sits still on her knees, her mouth open, and waits.

Nothing. Not a thought, or a sound, or even a retch.

"ForgetMeKnot," Kaleb murmurs, turning away too, looking sickened. If his face didn't tell me what he thought, his voice would.

I face my locker, wishing I could erase the secondhand experience from my mind. Mana is all kinds of fucked up. Mind, he must have seen what I did to his friend, and yet he did nothing to intervene. Who is the more disturbed in this hotel of mad fuckery? There's a song in that, somewhere.

"What do flowers have to do with this level of bullshit?" I whisper and rest my head against the cold locker door. The coolness helps, and I've overheated. Again.

Fuck, this is getting dangerous. Maybe I can't have the green-eyed girl after all. I certainly don't want to hurt her and I'm clearly unstable.

Kaleb laughs openly at me. "It's a drug. ForgetMeKnot. Like the dog thing where they get stuck together." He makes a lewd hand gesture, demonstrating the process.

My stomach turns. "Yeah, I got it. A drug, huh? What, it makes them submissive or some shit?"

"It makes them forget."

I rotate slowly toward him, grabbing my jeans and sliding them on. "Forget?"

"Everything. Before, after, during. Everything."

I stare at him, but Kaleb's attention is drawn to the door where a vision of auburn curls and eyes the color of the forest at dusk stops everything in the room. Even Alonzo's pathetic whimpers.

There's a drug I could use.

"Oh, God. Again?" She glares at Mana, stalking

forward and completely ignores the fact she and her drowned rat of a drugged-up sister are the only ones clothed within a sea of naked, predatory men.

And every single one of us want her. I scent their need in the air, even my own. Kaleb, drooling like that dog he mentioned. Mana. Especially Mana. His cock rises unashamedly as she approaches. "I can go again," he offers softly, and for the first time since I noticed him, he looks interested. Far more than when he shoved his horse cock down her sister's throat. "I can make it good." He reaches out, almost tenderly, to touch her face.

Like a professional boxer, Addi ducks and weaves, managing to avoid Mana's touch and extricate her sister with no small display of skill. She doesn't lose her footing once, and her glare fixed on Mana never wavers. *Girl's got balls.* I like that. Another thing I know about myself.

"Not for all the demons in hell, Mana. Keep your dick to yourself." She smiles sweetly through her snark and drags her sister away, muttering in an undertone. Addi pauses at the open doorway, and looks back. "And keep your drugs out of her too, you freak. If she wants to fuck, at least let her remember the experience, if she chooses. And if she doesn't..." The woodland sprite of a perfect spirit flicks her fingers between her eyes and Mana.

Without another word she leaves us all staring after the pair of them, the slut and the princess, and a different sound fills the room in their absence. Mana's laughter, akin to shattered glass shredding newborn flesh. After a moment, Kaleb reluctantly joins in, then me.

How much more fucked up can any of us be?

The funny thing is, we haven't even started.

JADE MARSHALL AND RAVEN HUSH

Chapter Five

The Little Green Monster

Adreana

I hate that I once again must be the person to fish my stupid sister out of the bowels of this decrepit building. What I hate even more is the fact that I have to watch Mana face-fuck her before I intervene. Jealousy thrums through me, and I feel dirty.

I can't stand the fucking man, but in this moment, I wish I were the one kneeling before him. Yes, I know that is insane but the libido wants what the libido wants. Also, I have never seen a cock like that in my life, not even in my late-night forays surfing porn sites. My mind spins with thoughts of being stuffed with the intimidating member and I have to press my thighs together to stave off my arousal.

"I can go again," Mana says softly, his dark eyes burning into me as he reaches out to touch my face.

I dodge him, not wanting his touch after seeing him defile my sister. How many others have there been tonight? He doesn't seem like a one-woman man.

"I can make it good," he tries to tempt me.

I watch the girth hanging between his thighs kick to life, straining in my direction. Dear God, I'm sure that monster cock would rip me in two. The thing that bothers me is I can't decide if I would more likely beg for mercy … or for more. My brain hurts every time I think about Mana, and the thin line between lust and hate I walk when it comes to him.

"Not for all the demons in hell, Mana. Keep your dick to yourself." I smile sweetly even though my tone is anything but. I pause at the open doorway and give him a dirty look. "And keep your drugs out of her too, you freak. If she wants to fuck, at least let her remember. And if she doesn't..." I want to threaten him, but I know anything I throw at him will fall on deaf ears. Instead, I flick my fingers between my eyes and Mana.

The message is clear: *I'll be watching.*

Without another word I wrap my arm around my sister's middle and walk us both out of there. The sound of Mana's dark laughter follows us before the others join in.

It's the third time I have had to retrieve my sister like some lost puppy. Tomorrow, she won't have a single recollection of the entire event and she will fawn endlessly about Mana. I know she believes if she can only get him to fuck her, she can lay a claim to one of the most powerful and feared men in Oregon.

I know better.

Mana simply sees her as another hole to fill. Or another hole to shove his drool-worthy monster cock into. I have yet to walk in on him actually fucking her. I wonder if that is because he isn't interested, like Kaleb, or if I just catch them before he can get to the main event every time. The man surely has the stamina to go for another round if what I saw earlier was any indication.

Stuffing my stoned sister into the back seat of my little metallic blue Honda Civic, I drive home, taking my time. My thoughts are muddled with lust and laced with the little bit of fear remaining from the bathroom incident the hour before.

If I had been able to find Emma, she never would have ended up on her knees for Mana tonight. But of course, the vapid little bitch was nowhere to be found. I searched high and low before I located her. Once again, she left me high and dry, and I had to deal with what happened on my own.

I can be grateful that the stoic blonde giant was there to save me or this night could have gone so much worse. Kaleb offered to drive me home, his breath teasing my skin as he stared right through me with those luminous eyes. Maybe I should have taken him up on the offer?

But I wanted my sister. Not the woman in the back of my car, the woman who tries to use her body to get ahead in life. No, I wanted my twin, the girl who survived with me when our parents died, who laughed and cried with me for years. I want the comfort of someone that no longer exists. I realize how stupid that sounds but after nearly being sexually assaulted and watching a man die, that's exactly what I wanted.

Parking in front of the faded green door of our garage, I shut off the engine and rest my head on the steering wheel. Taking a deep breath, I gather myself from the verge of tears before stepping out. Glaring through the back window, I take in the woman that is no longer my sister.

"You can either get yourself in the house or sleep in the fucking car," I say loudly. "I am so fucking done with you."

And I am. Tomorrow, one of us will be vacating the house and I am guessing it will be her. I have saved up enough money in the last three years doing website designs and working hours at the diner that I can afford to buy her out of her half of the house.

Emma, on the other hand, hasn't held a job for more than two weeks at a time. She will be more than happy to take my money.

I don't enter through the front door but walk around the side to make my way in from the back. The moment I have the side gate open, Daisy assaults me with her hyper pit bull brand of affection, laving me with kisses.

"I'm happy to see you too, girl." I laugh, scratching behind her ears. "Let's go to bed. We'll deal with all this other shit in the morning."

Daisy barks before bolting for the back door. Standing on the wooden porch, her entire body wiggles with excitement and I can't hold back my smile. Daisy really is the highlight of my life.

"Do you only smile like that at dogs?"

The question comes from the darkened edge of the house. A loud shriek falls from my lips and Daisy starts barking. She is in front of me, the hair on her neck standing straight up as she protects me.

"Whoa," the voice says again before Kaleb steps into the circle of light falling from the naked bulb above my back porch. "I didn't mean to scare you."

He stares at me intently as I try to calm Daisy. "Shh, girl. It's okay." I stroke her fur and give her extra attention until she settles and stops barking. She doesn't take her eyes off Kaleb, and I know one wrong move will have her ripping a chuck out of him. She has always been overprotective of me.

The feeling of being watched settles over me and after everything that has happened tonight, I finally feel peace. This is what I wanted from my sister. Strange how someone I've never met can offer me the comfort she no longer does.

"What are you doing here, Kaleb?" I ask, stepping closer to the back door. I don't know this man, and suddenly I don't feel as comfortable around him.

"I wanted to check up on you," he says with a shrug that seems out of place on a man his size. "I know tonight has been a lot. First the bathroom, and then Mana and Emma."

A dark, emotionless laugh falls from my lips. "A lot?" He has the decency to look sheepish. "Yes, Kaleb. I'm fine. Thank you for stopping by to check on me." I wonder how he looked up our address, then stop wondering. Emma was all over him earlier.

He nods, making his way closer to me. Daisy growls lowly, but doesn't do anything yet. His hand caresses my cheek, his gaze taking in every feature of my face.

"And I wanted to do this."

He doesn't give me a chance to pull away before his lips land on mine. His kiss is forceful but allows me the space to pull away if I want. But I don't want to. I also want to be reckless and throw caution to the wind. What could one kiss hurt?

So, I give in, twining my arms behind his neck and pulling him closer. Kaleb palms my ass, pulling my body flush with his. Fuck, this man can kiss.

Kaleb pulls away, breathing just as harshly as I am. "Damn, girl."

I shake my head, words lost to me. What the hell just happened?

"I want to take you on a date," he says with a devilish grin. "Say yes, please."

"What?"

"One date." He massages the globe of my ass he has yet to let go of, staring into my eyes. "If you don't like me, we can go our separate ways. But there is something about you I can't put my finger on, something that calls to me, and I hope you'll give me a chance to figure out what it is."

"I don't know," I say, stepping from his grip.

"You won't know until you give me a chance."

"I do my best to stay away from Harken, Mana, and anyone associated with him," I reply honestly. "I

51

have enough problems dealing with Emma. I don't need to add drug dealers and assholes into the mix."

"Then I'll quit," Kaleb replies.

"Being a drug dealer or an asshole?"

"Either. Both. Whatever it takes."

I stare at him with my mouth hanging open. "You can't be serious."

"I am. I don't need to work at Harken. I do it because I'm bored."

"You'll give up your job for a single date? What if we don't get along?"

"Sweetness, I'm positive you and I are going to get along like a house on fire." His grin has returned.

I watch him carefully. I'm trying to figure out if he is serious but he isn't giving away a damn thing.

"If you lie to me and I find out—" I start, but he cuts me off.

"I never lie."

Chapter Six

I Got a Date with a Hot Girl

Kaleb

She said yes and now I have a date. Not with just any girl—*the* girl. The one I know will knock me on my ass until the day I put a ring on her finger, and then she'll knock me down some more.

I whistle into the wind, my tuneless song fading in my wake as I wander away from her house. Leaving might have been the hardest thing I've ever done, but after hoisting her drug-fucked sister out of her Honda Civic—damn, that would be the first present I buy my girl, a new car—any thoughts of taking that kiss that rocked my cock earlier fucked right off.

Emma drooled a little Mana on me, and nothing could take that edge of pure, from the source, ForgetMeKnot, off. Not even a scalding shower followed by an icy one in their shared upstairs bathroom. The place stinks of Harken's drug, and Addi. It's like Mana personally marked up her private space, and I swear I'll eradicate every damn inch of him from that house as soon as I get a key.

As in, the one she will give me maybe three sleepovers in once I kiss her senseless, make her breakfast, and show her what real love feels like. Not the key that fit her lock just fine that I made from her sister's key ring a month prior. The place draws me to it, and I thought for a while it had something to do with the location... Now I know it's who lives inside the Gothic mansion that calls to me.

And I can give Addi so much more than watching her from the shadows. Not that I'm the only one who watches her, but I'll be the one to claim her, give her so much more than the shit show Mana exposed her to. That man—I *know* he isn't human, but he pays fine and I give my loyalty to my employers—brings *toxic* to another level in so many ways. Fuck, his blood has half the damn town high most weekends.

I have no intention of letting him any closer to Addi than necessary. Her sister … well, I'm not beyond giving up a little sacrifice for the cause. And her twin doesn't seem impressed to have to drag her out of Harken yet again.

My footsteps never falter as I turn toward Mana's doorstep, already planning the strategy I need to take. What I don't count on is the extra set of footsteps that fall in line at my side.

"Would you like to tell him, or shall I?" a deceptively soft voice purrs. Bowen Kathros. Mana's keeper, and kept pet.

The tall angel keeps pace with me easily. Heat rockets off the man who waltzes around in a white wifebeater, squiggly marks he manages to pass off as ink adorning every inch of his marred skin. Pale gray hair drapes artistically over his equally pale face, all angles and harsh lines that if you look at just right doesn't look so perfect after all.

But only if you catch the angel off guard.

"I'll fight my own battles, thanks." I learned long ago to watch the bargains I make around immortals who play at being men, like those who made them never threw them out of their realms for whatever reasons.

Since no one told me, I guess they were all really shit at their jobs to be forced into a human existence with each other for company.

"I can be your backup."

"Ever the temptress." I pause at the edge of Sinner's End land, aiming for the shortcut back to Harken through the town, instead of around the people I know Bowen will want to avoid. "I wonder, do you bend over on Sundays as well, or would I be better to place my money with you on the corner?" I eye him with a shit-eating grin. "I'll buy you a pretty skirt."

Bowen looks sickened when he sees my intended route, and I know his greenage has nothing to do with my teasing. For all his pomp and presence, all his showy "look at me" bullshit, he's an outright coward.

"I happen to look fabulous in drag," he murmurs, wiggling his ass a little in the white leather pants he habitually wears.

I swear he and Mana, with his longer, dark hair, look like a nineties' boy band duet. Not that I'd say so, because I happen to like my dick attached to my body.

"Of course you do." I shake my head. "Was *anything* off limits wherever the hell you came from?"

The grin he throws my way and the heated glance that travels south dissolves my smile. "Not half as much as they make out down here. Gender norms aren't as rigid." He leans across me, swiping his fingers over my dick that hardens against my will. "Mmm, your desire for the pretty little fire flower at Sinner's End does it for you, doesn't she?"

I clench my teeth and keep walking. "I never said you could touch."

Bowen withdraws his hand, disappointment flitting through his strangely colorless eyes that reflect the night in a pool of liquid diamond starlight. "Pity. We could have had some fun. I do love a good role-play."

"Not gonna kink shame you, bro. But that's my date, and I'll take the real skin over..." I replay the once-over he gave me a moment before, "over something fake."

Bowen's nostrils flare at the insult I don't bother to veil. "Have it your way. Mana is all yours. I'll watch from above." He darts away to … somewhere.

I don't bother to look up. The heavy updraught that slides seductively along my body like a warm breath is unwelcome enough to leave me wishing I wore my leather jacket on a stiflingly hot night.

"And stay the fuck away," I mutter for good measure.

So much for the facade of being human. I doubt he can hear me, but I curse anyway, letting my mouth run on as I consider which part of my soul Mana is likely to shred first, or if that's beyond his reach until after my death. Seeing as it was my mouth that landed me in his employ in the first place, it seems apt.

My path through the town is fast, mostly as I know once daylight hits the structure Mana will be dead to the world and I'll have to wait until the next evening before I can make good on my promise to Addi. That isn't happening, because I want her body pressed to mine again too damn bad.

The way she kissed me back, her soft lips parting against the push of my tongue, how she wrapped her hands around my neck and pulled me closer … her ass in my hand—she is a one-hand grip for sure, both sides, and—*fuckkkk.*

If I don't stop replaying the feel of her curves pressed to my body, I'll never be in the right mindset to face Mana. That's a fight I need to have full control of, because the bastard fights dirty. Real fucking dirty.

****

"He's not here." Lethe stands sentry outside his master's office, his back as rigid as anyone's I've ever seen, and that's saying something for a kid who was taught by nuns.

"Bullshit." I raise a hand to knock but an arm made of pure metal, I swear, blocks my path. I raise both my eyebrows. "Excuse me?"

Lethe looks me full in the face. "No one enters, and he's not here."

"You're a real broken record, aren't you?" I snap, letting my irritation eke out on the man in the black leather pants and no shirt. Starry patterns decorate his torso and I narrow my eyes as I study him, until it finally clicks. "Like Bowen," I murmur softly.

"Who?" Lethe frowns at me.

"Nothing." I incline my head, but not in a show of obedience.

Something is off about this man apart from his rigid stance. He might have just started working for Mana, but the way he stands like a toy soldier waiting to be wound, it's like he can't function without commands. Like he doesn't know who he is. Or what.

"That's fair." Lethe looks straight past me down the hall.

I blink at the revelation. "Have you tried the merchandise?" I raise both eyebrows and give them a waggle. "The drugs," I add more softly when he remains silent.

Lethe still stares over my head. Looking for … absolution? A sign? Fuck knows.

"Okay. Well, I'll be off finding the boss. Unless you've got any ideas where I can start?" I pivot on my heel, keen to get the fuck away from the silent sentinel who gives off no vibes whatsoever. Like he's a void. An abyss where energy falls endlessly, never to emerge.

The faster I'm out of this place, the better.

"Try the bell tower. He seemed to like its height." The soft voice at my back surprises me, but not in the way Lethe might expect.

No, you poor pure, untouched thing. It's because of the souls who dived from the top. He can hear their fatal cries there best. But I don't say that, and he doesn't talk again, or breathe or anything else I can tell as my steps quicken in the direction of the belfry.

Because like a twisted Gothic gargoyle, I know Mana will be at the very top, staring out at what he can't have, listening to the music of the suffering shades plummeting and twisting below in their endless torment. A symphony made for a devil.

But I can.

Which makes this next interaction dangerous as fuck. Because not only does my boss—soon-to-be ex-boss—play dirty, he's a damn sore loser too. And he loses about as often as I lie.

Never.

Not because I choose not to, I literally can't make a lie fall out of my mouth. It became such a habit as a child that I stopped trying, which means I need to hold to that promise I made Addi or become a liar through omission—and that seems like a fairly shithouse way to start a relationship.

She thinks she might annoy me. That she might not like something about me. But the way she reacted to me in Harken's underbelly, how she kissed me back at her house … there is nothing objectionable between us, and that is exactly how it will stay.

My boots pound the scarred flagstone steps, my blood heating as I complete circuit after circuit up the winding staircase. The echoes that fill the tower deafen me, an easy warning to the boss man of my presence, though after tonight he will cease to have any hold over me.

Good.

He's been my keeper for long enough during my short tenure at Harken, the reason I don't make deals with demons or angels or gods or fucking toadstools. Who knows what might bite me in the ass at some future point?

I've spent enough time in Harken to know the walls contain something worse than brick and mortar, and the inhabitants are just as cruel and tortured as those of its violent past.

"Can you try to make less noise? You might wake the dead with that ruckus," Mana calls as I near the top step, tucking his semi-thickened cock back into his leather pants and pulling the crotch strings until they squeal.

"Were you pissing or wanking?" I mutter, forcing my gaze to remain steady on his face. Anything else will be seen as weakness, and I have no doubt Mana sees far more than I will ever wish him to see.

"Does it matter?" He shrugs and gives his covered cock a rough squeeze.

I feel the touch like his hand is on my crotch instead of his own, and the second squeeze is gentler. *Caressing.* "Stop that," I hiss, slamming my knuckles against the belfry's stonework. The pain helps a little, but my cock still hardens. "You do not have my consent."

Maybe it's me who sounds like the broken record.

Mana stares at me, the corners of his mouth crooking up in a sly smile that douses me in ice everywhere other than where his phantom touch rests. "Is that so? Consent is a funny thing. I don't remember you requesting to leave the premises this evening either, but you did, didn't you? I think you took something from me."

He rubs his cock, the leather straining as he swells. The man has endless endurance in his corner. My cock receives the same attention and salutes the unwelcome, ghostly touch no matter how much I hate the man and what he can do to me.

"I took nothing that wasn't yours to start with," I grate out. I slam my palms to the walls and drag my nails along the rough-hewn surface, staining it with streaks of my blood.

Mana hums his approval, his eyes hooding. "Don't stop me. Not if you want me to release you."

Phantom fingers brush my balls, tantalizingly sweet and gentle, like her—I banish the thought and let out an unwilling howl at the invasion on my favorite fantasy. Addi on her knees, my cock buried deep in her throat as I stroke her hair gently when she sobs for me, her fingertips stroking the underside of my balls until I rupture in her mouth.

The touch disappears and I drop to my knees, panting. Blood still roars in my ears as I slump over the stone, breath shuddering from my chest.

"You fucking asshole."

"I've been called worse." I can *hear* the smile in Mana's voice.

"I don't doubt you've earned it."

"Well, yes. But that's the fun part, isn't it? Look what you're giving up if you walk away." His voice hardens.

I laugh, though there's no humor in it. "You make it sound like I have a choice." I slowly force myself to stand once more, knowing this is far from over.

"Don't you?"

His touch is back though his hands are well away from his body. The bulge in his pants remains, and I wonder how many more club slut throats he'll jam his cock down tonight before he's satisfied. Mana constantly chases the high, never acknowledging what any drug addict could tell him: the first high is the best. And the worst.

It's a curse in itself, one that's forever chased after and never met again, always culminating in a cycle of disappointment and self-loathing.

"Don't drag me into your shit." Raising my chin, I hold his gaze. "Do your worst, Manashesh Severn. If I walk away, she's mine. You leave her alone. Forever."

"Such stark terms." Ghost fingers travel around my cock, squeezing enough to make my length strain for more, yet not enough to give me the climax aching through me. "Should I accept his demands, Bowen?"

"I think you should let me take care of that pain you feel." Bowen appears at the edge of the bell tower's arch, crouching there in his bare feet and white leather pants and singlet like he flew in.

Fuck knows if he did.

Wait—did he say *pain*?

"As long as you stay standing, you will have what you desire." Mana's voice breaks through my train of thought, but not enough to distract me from that little gem.

Pain. Is that what Mana feels when he comes? I stare past the devil tormenting me to the angel balancing delicately on his toes at the edge of nothingness. One push would send him plummeting seven floors to the soul-stained ground where more suicides and murders have taken place than any other spot on the premises.

Harken's history is a temptation to the horror inside Mana, everything he needs to feed on. Power. Greed. Now, sex can be added to that list.

Bowen smiles at me through his lashes and I

swear he exposes tiny motherfucking fangs in my direction.

Whoever said angels are fat, happy-faced babies is a fucking liar. They are the most dangerous beings in the universe—or at least, the ones who roam Harken certainly are.

Taking the information as the gift intended, I give in to Mana's touch, letting the first groan rip from my throat. The sounds seem to please him, and his hand wanders back to the front of his pants only to be knocked away by Bowen.

"Allow me," the angel whispers, dropping to his knees and reaching for the laces at the front of Mana's bulge.

Mana catches the angel's face in a cruel pincer grip, holding him at bay. "Mouth only over my pants. You don't get the privilege of swallowing me whole."

Bowen pouts sensually. "But you let the sluts fill their faces with your cum," he whines, writhing on his haunches.

Damn, the man puts on one hell of a show.

"And they will forget the experience. Something I can't take from you." Mana releases his face and cups the back of the pale man's neck. "Lips and tongue only. No teeth tonight." His head falls back as Bowen's mouth rubs over his bulge.

The angel's tongue flicks out to trace his horse cock, and I have the privilege of experiencing every tormenting lick secondhand as though his mouth warms my own crotch. Mana's touch doesn't disappear, and the dual contact is far more than I can bear, especially when the angel seals his mouth over the other man's leathers and *breathes*.

My cry shatters the silence gathering around the blood-marked place, and with a quick flick of hands and tongue I come undone, disgracing myself in my pants with the illicitness—and the impossibility—of it all.

My knees shake and I stumble forward, but Mana's words ricochet in my head. *As long as you stay standing..."*

A scream builds in me as the hands and mouth never stop, running endlessly over my throbbing, aching, overstimulated cock. I harden again and again, screaming with every sweet kiss Bowen bestows upon his master, every hard jerk Mana's phantom touch gives my cock when I slide back into the realm of pleasure, his pain becoming my own.

My jeans are drenched with ropes of cum, the walls painted with my blood where my nails tear jagged against raw fingertips.

And as the sun crests the walls of Harken Asylum we scream together, welcoming the dawn in a tandem of torment. I stand still, knees locked, cum leaking down my thighs. My cock is rubbed raw, and I'm still moaning as Bowen brings us both to the edge and over again.

I don't fall until the sun has risen beyond the walls, the golden orb witness to my torture as I tumble to my knees, my vow to Mana fulfilled.

I remained standing all night.

She is mine.

JADE MARSHALL AND RAVEN HUSH

Chapter Seven

Small Favors

Mana

My ears still ring from the screams of hours before. This time at least only half of them are mine. I swallow on a raw throat as I pry my eyes open on a darkened belfry. *Thanks, Bowen, for dragging my ass somewhere safe.* It looks like the angel left me where I fell afterward, exposed and unable to provide my usual dose for the Chemist in the basement. Like that's a normality I can accept, that I have accepted for the past decade or more.

A harsh laugh ripples its way along my damaged throat. Yes, because that's an experience I look forward to daily. The entire setup sounds like a horrific manga.

And this is the human existence I garnered for myself.

The loss of Kaleb, the human Renfield who would have shouldered my dead weight—pun intended—back to ground level, deeper as required, after his torture at my hands is a deficit I don't want to ruminate upon.

All over a girl. *The* girl. The one who consumes us all.

Except maybe Lethe, seeing as he hasn't had the pleasure of tasting her fear as often, though he was present when she towed her pathetic facsimile of a sister from the showers last night. No two girls so different inside should look so similar on the outside.

One with moss green eyes the color of a forest at dusk, stunning auburn locks like silken ties that could wind a soul in and tether him to her like a belonging … a pet. Something I knew any one of us would rent our existence apart to become. To possess. Because if she possesses one of us, we will own her, too.

Kaleb thinks he's won the prize, but he didn't consider all the elements of my deal. I know he believes I required him to stand throughout the night to fulfill his bargain, but he failed to consider my earlier wording. He fell first, and that puts him back in my … what do the humans say? My *bad books*.

How apt.

I smile at the rising moon and slither down the stairs, wondering what the seven-story drop would do to this form if I took the leap. Would I lie there, shattered on the hard-packed dirt floor until this body repaired itself? A feature of the asylum itself. Another soul for the grounds to claim. This land and the hallowed grounds at Sinner's End provide the entirety of my domain on this earth. This realm.

I should have begged for more from my creator. Perhaps that's why I'm so harsh in my dealings in this place. Because I was so desperate to leave that I forgot to negotiate in full.

Why should I do any less for the desperate souls that frequent Harken? Clinging to that remnant of control, I find the basement door and push it open to find the Chemist waiting for me. Alonzo's sharp gaze misses nothing.

"Thanks for coming to retrieve me," I murmur, unable to keep the pettiness from my voice.

I turn my back to the human and wince. The leathers draw too tight across my cock where the angel broke his promise and sank his fangs into my balls, draining me in an inhumane way, and a totally unsatisfactory conclusion to our … foray.

Kaleb's face, on the other hand—I'd never been sure if he swung both ways, but from the way his body reacted to our touches, I suspected he kept more than one internal door shut in his obsession for the girl who clouds our vision.

Perhaps we can take turns wining and dining the pretty piece of fluff, then fuck her together, and play with each other after.

The image keeps me mostly sane as the Chemist digs into my veins with his endless supplies of needles and drains me in another way.

****

"You let her wander away," I whisper, my voice still a ruin a mere three hours later.

Lethe stands on the other side of my desk, his back as straight as though I hold him that way on marionette strings. Mind, if I held up a puppet, the strings would be a tangled mess of half-broken promises and twisted orders that turned back on themselves over and over again.

"I saved her innocence." He stares over my head like he can't stand to be here, but has nowhere else to go. A truth, though I don't appreciate either his candor or his distance.

I snort. "That girl fucks herself with a toy every night and spreads the fluids of her sin across her bed to sleep in. I can hear her all the way down in the bowels of this prison I've made for myself."

Under our watchful eyes. Does she know how many otherworldly beings observe her nightly behavior? I could swear she's drawing us in, a tempting little morsel of bait on the end of a short line.

Not that I can even enter her house until one of

the sisters either invites me or is in mortal peril, enough that I can break the bonds of the agreement on that land. It stands on the other side of my boundary, inside the line of hallowed ground where the cemetery resides. Does she know how the souls call to me? How *hers* sings louder the closer we are? It's a beautiful melody of torture and wanting, of predator and prey.

When I fucked her sister's mouth the night before, I imagined Adreana's mouth latched around my cock, choking on it. I can't forget that it's not her who swallowed me, letting me bruise her slender throat, or choke her until I constricted my hand around my cock through the thin membrane of her flesh.

I can't forget, even though I left the other girl with no memory. Another puppet to play with.

What began as a game has devilled into boredom. I need a new puzzle. One with auburn hair and moss green eyes. One I'll play with and make her *remember*.

If I have to exist within my pool of torment, so will she. I want to see her eyes flare wide, her mouth stuffed with this body's flesh as I moan through the pleasure laced with pain and my cum jets down onto her stomach.

I will watch her writhe with the orgasm the act gives her, because that's what my fluids do.

One to forget. One giving pleasure.

Both are a cursed promise. Once tasted, it's an addiction. I have to make the endless line of nightly toys forget, else they'd be ravenous, clambering over me.

I only want to do that to one female, and my restless day's sleep on the bell tower's stone balcony was filled with the torture of knowing she was near and not being able to touch her. All the while she was at her strange house with its ridiculous caveats and deals that tether her so far from me, yet close enough to taste.

Maybe I should bargain for the restrictions on that land to be reduced. How many years would that shave off my penance here, or would it add to them? Did it matter? It's not like I'm intent on marrying the girl. I want to possess her, be who she craves, what she wants every minute of every day. I want her begging for my cock, to train her mouth to flood with saliva the moment I put her hand on my crotch.

Perhaps she and Bowen can serve me together.

Twisting the angel's purpose—knowing he also craves her—that eases the hurt within me. And like any addict, it still isn't enough.

I need more.

My fist slams onto my desk, leaving a large dent in the hardwood surface. "Bring her to me."

Lethe doesn't so much as flinch as he offers a sharp nod and strides out of my office with purpose.

It's been a damn long time since I moved like that. Finally letting my guard down in the absence of prying eyes that might foresee the show of weakness as what it is, I slump in my seat, letting out a heartfelt groan. Fuck this form. I'm too weak, too human.

I almost envy Lethe in his ability to forget everything.

A demented smile etches my face. "Lethe," I call softly, though the walls echo my words to perfection, obeying the single command of pure thought: *bring him back to me.*

Lethe returns to my office, pausing with a single toe of his bared foot over the threshold. "Yes?"

His imperious tone brings me to my feet. I fist my hands until hot fluid coats my fingers and runs between them. The scent of burning sulphur fills my office.

"Fuck with her date first." I breathe hard through my nose. *And show a little obsequience.*

"I beg your pardon?" Lethe's brow dips.

"You heard." I let the growl rend the air between us in a threat I'm not entirely certain I can carry out right now. From the disdainful look on Lethe's face, neither is he.

"You want me to … mess with her?" he asks slowly.

"Is such an order beneath you?"

He blinks, and his face clears. "No, sir," he says softly. "Who is the date?"

"Kaleb."

A hard smile lights his face. "My pleasure."

In a swift turn on his heels, he's gone.

I lean back in my chair and smile.

Chapter Eight

Date Night

Adreana

I sit in front of the vanity that used to belong to my mother staring at myself in the mirror, into green eyes that also belonged to her. Sometimes it hurts to look at myself since I look so much like her. Emma has long since changed her appearance so drastically she barely resembles the woman who gave birth to us. I've even caught her wearing blue contact lenses.

How can one person want so badly to be someone she isn't? It hurts my head just trying to figure it out.

Emma glares at me from the doorway, leaning against the wooden frame.

"So, you're kicking me out of the only house I've ever known?" She is trying to push my buttons, but I won't let her.

"No. I am offering to buy your half. At market value might I add," I reply, swiping mascara across my lashes. "Please stop pretending you give a shit about this house, or me for that matter. We both know you would rather be anywhere else in the world. You don't belong here."

"Don't you dare judge me, Adreana."

No one calls me by my full name, but she is trying to remind me that no one knows me better than she does. What she seems to forget is that I know her just as well and I can see through her ruse.

"I'm not judging," I say, looking directly at her. "I am merely stating the facts as we both know them to be.

You've always believed you were too good for this house, this life, and whatever is left of this family."

She looks like I've slapped her. It's the first real emotion I've seen in ages and I almost feel bad. But I can't constantly put my life on hold for my sister, especially if she isn't willing to do the same for me.

"Just take the money and go," I say, returning my attention to the mirror. "I don't care what you do anymore. Chase after Mana, or whoever. Just know that I will be changing the locks come morning."

"Addi," she says softly, drawing my attention. "You know I love you, right?"

She looks like a sixteen-year-old for a moment, and I almost cave. But I can't forget all the shit she has put me through in the past couple of years.

"I know you love me, Em. But sometimes love isn't enough. You don't like or respect me and to be blunt, I feel the same way. So, I think it's time we cut our losses."

The doorbell rings, drawing her attention from our conversation. Before I can stop her, she is already out of my room and heading downstairs.

I know who is on the other side of the door and I was rather hoping Emma would be gone before he showed up. But true to his text, it's seven o'clock and he's here to pick me up for our date.

"You're looking fine," Emma says in a sultry tone.

I walk down the stairs slowly, listening to their conversation.

"Thank you," Kaleb says, but I can hear the edge to his voice.

"What brings you around here? I'll be at Harken later tonight." Emma flirts.

"First, you need to stop touching me." Anger

laces his words. "I didn't consent to you putting your hands on me. Second, I'm here to take Addi out."

"Addi?"

"Yes, your sister."

"Addi?"

It's like the girl doesn't understand English all of a sudden, and I want to smack her. It isn't that hard to understand. Stepping up beside her, I smile at the man who begged and bartered for this opportunity.

My nerves get the better of me and I run my sweaty hands over my stonewashed skinny jeans. I didn't know where he wanted to take me tonight so I kept it pretty but casual. Skinny jeans, black pumps, and a flowy white and slate gray blouse that shows off my shoulders.

"Wow!" he says with a smile the moment he sees me. "You're looking stunning, sweetness."

An unwanted blush spreads across my cheeks. I swear to all that's holy I am trying to keep my cool, but it's not easy when a guy like Kaleb pays you attention. It feels like a caress as he skims his gaze over every inch of me. Not that he is hard on the eyes, either.

Dark jeans and a fitted, bright blue t-shirt show off all the muscles he hides in his work uniform. And that smile is enough to have grown women swooning.

"Adreana," Emma says beside me. "What's going on?"

I roll my eyes so hard I worry they might get stuck. Again, with this first name bullshit? "I told you I was going on a date," I say, hoping she'll drop the situation.

"With a guy you knew I had a thing for?" She crosses her arms under her breasts, forcing them higher on her chest, her powder pink tank top leaving little to the imagination. She isn't wearing a bra, and the fabric is almost see-through.

I give Kaleb a side look to assess whether he is staring only to find him standing beside his matte black muscle car.

"Do we really need to do this now?" I ask. "You don't really want Kaleb. You're just pissed he doesn't want you."

My sister steps into my personal space, rage burning in her emerald gaze that is so much like mine. "We're done." Malice drips from every word out of her mouth. "I'll make sure to be gone whenever you get home with your new fuck toy."

She makes sure her words are loud enough for Kaleb to hear. Maybe if he thinks I'm like her, he'll be less interested in me ... then neither of us will have him.

"Fine." I sigh, walking away. "I'll wire the money in the morning."

But Emma doesn't hear my words as she slams the front door. I'm sure she is going to break a bunch of shit just to let me know how angry she really is. And I'll have to go through all my stuff to assess what she's taken with her. But I'm finally free.

I know that sounds super fucked-up, but all I want is to breathe. To live. To be myself without constantly having to raise a whore-woman who acts like a spoiled fucking child. She wants to act like a grown-up when life is going well but throws tantrums like a toddler the moment anything doesn't go her way. I'm done acting like a parent. It's time to start living my own life.

"Are you okay?" Kaleb asks as he holds the passenger side door open for me. "We can do this another night."

I place a kiss on his cheek. "You wanted a date. Show me what you got, handsome."

I slide into the seat, buttery-soft leather holding me in place. It's divine. And exactly what I need right now. Kaleb hops in and cranks the engine, allowing the V8 to roar to life. Damn, my dad would have loved this car.

I shake off the melancholy threatening to overcome me. "Where are we going?"

"Sweetness, anywhere you want," he says and chuckles. "I don't actually have a plan, I just want to spend time with you."

I grin at his words. Never has anyone said anything like this to me. It's flattering and overwhelming at the same time. Damn, there goes that blush again.

"What's your favorite food?" Kaleb asks. "And for all that's holy please don't say tofu."

"And if I do?" I ask with a straight face.

The look of horror on his face has me bursting into giggles.

"Then we'll eat tofu and rabbit food for dinner," he replies with a grimace as he tries his best to hide his smile.

"Dear God, just not that," I say smiling in return. "I'm a red meat girl. Steak and burgers make me happy."

"Is that what it takes to make you truly happy?" he asks, suddenly serious.

"No. Bacon and coffee make me truly happy. But you can start with a decent burger."

****

The date is going better than I expected. Kaleb stopped at a little burger shack I've never seen before and got us each a big bacon and cheeseburger, fries, and a milkshake. Then he drove to the bank of the Willamette River where we've been sitting for the better part of an hour, eating our burgers and not talking about any damn thing in particular.

I have learned a few things about Kaleb, though.

He is rich, like stupid rich. His mother died when he was three and left him a mega trust fund, but he doesn't like people to know. He has been taken advantage of many times before and doesn't want it to happen again. So, he works as a bartender and lives in a modest apartment. Just like any other normal guy in Portland.

I know he prefers quality over quantity. Food, drink, friends. He would rather have one great thing than ten mediocre things.

And lastly, he loves dogs. Which would have been a deal-breaker for me if he didn't. I thought he was lying, but he showed me some photos on his phone of his previous pooch.

"I haven't felt right getting a new dog," he explained. "Not just because I still miss my buddy, Marshall. But because I spend more time at Harken than at home. It just wouldn't have been fair."

"I understand that," I reply with a smile. "But I don't know what I would do without Daisy."

He laughs at the videos I have on my phone. Daisy chasing butterflies, Daisy stealing apples from the tree in the yard. Daisy just being a regular, hyperactive pittie.

A cold wind blows over us, and a shiver works its way down my spine.

"Mana wants to see you."

"Fuck!" I yell, falling off the hood of Kaleb's muscle car. Glaring up, I see the man who saved me from being assaulted last night.

Kaleb's anger radiates off him in waves. "I told Mana I was done. We had an agreement."

"Not you," the muscular blond replies, nodding in my direction.

Kaleb helps me up as I glare. "I don't have a

damn thing to do with Mana, and certainly nothing to say to him."

"Why are you here, Lethe?" Kaleb asks.

Lethe? What a strange fucking name. Actually, it suits the strange man.

"Mana sent me," he replies, sounding robotic. I wonder if he is also sampling the drug supply at Harken. "Be glad I'm being decent. Well, I think I am." He frowns in confusion, flexing his hands at his sides. "He wanted me to fuck with your date."

"What?" I demand.

"But you looked so happy, smiling with Kaleb," he says softly. "I didn't want that to end."

My heart breaks a little for him. He reminds me of Daisy when I first adopted her. Wanting to be loyal but not quite sure what was expected of her. I wonder what happened to this mountain of a man to make him look so terribly fucking lost.

"Tell Mana I'll be there at ten."

Lethe looks doubtful. I smile, hoping to reassure him.

"Fine." And then he walks off into the surrounding trees, disappearing into the dark.

"You don't have to do this," Kaleb says, drawing me against his chest and hugging me tightly.

"I need to make him understand that he doesn't own me. He and Emma can do whatever they want. But I am done with both of them and that fucking asylum he calls home."

Chapter Nine

First Date Expectations

Kaleb

Addi looks so damn pretty when she's angry— prettier than ever—so what the fuck does that say about me? But I'm not here to talk about me. It's her I want, in every way. Her scent wrapped around me, her body tight beneath mine as I show her what love really is.

Yeah, I fall hard and fast, but I've kept this part of me locked away for so long, from so many breaches of trust that delved soul-deep that I wasn't sure I could want someone this way again.

Mission achieved, asshole.

Her head rests on my shoulder as I pull her back onto the hood of my car, tipping her head back to stare up at the night's early stars. Her eyes are half-closed, her body soft where she curves into my embrace. I love that look on her face, her lips soft, the tension of a moment before gone. *Trust.* The one thing I crave, and she gives it to me freely. This girl will break me, I know she will.

And I'm not running.

I trace my knuckles along the gentle slope of her jaw. Her lips part on a breath that's sweet and heady and leaves me as hard as granite. I shift her onto my lap, wanting her to know the effect her proximity has on me and needing her closer all at once.

"You're handsy, aren't you?" she murmurs, the easy way we were before Lethe's intrusion sliding back. It better fucking stay too, because if I get her in my arms for a few hours, she's *mine*.

"I need to touch you." I don't hide the desire that leaves my voice ragged at the edges. Why shouldn't I be honest if she can give me her trust that fast?

She frowns, her gaze refocusing on me as she tips her head back farther. "Is this a marking-your-territory thing after that asshole turned up? I mean, a pretty asshole, and a confused one, but still. I'm here with *you*."

I swallow hard. "Yeah. You are." Without any more thought about it, and as natural as can be, I dip my head and brush my mouth over hers.

Pleasure sings through my veins as if she is made for me, and I'm here for every goddamn drop of it. When she and that toxic-as-fuck sister of hers came into the asylum—let's be real about where Mana keeps his secrets—I thought she was bait for him. Hell, maybe she still is. But she seemed untouchable and that made me want her more.

Addi freezes, the soft lines of her body stiffening as I suck in a controlled breath and go back for seconds. Because I'm a greedy mother, and I need to taste her, make sure she remembers the taste of *me* tonight when she lies in her bed and slips her hands between her thighs. Not Mana, and sure as fuck not Lethe, who she seemed to form an instant connection with. Just me.

Fuck, she's right. I am claiming her because he looked at her that way, like he wanted to take her home. Or worse, like he wanted *her* to take *him* home.

My head swirls with too many thoughts as her lips part the slightest amount. It's more than I need to drive my tongue into her mouth, cupping the back of her head. The softness disappears from us both, transforming into something raging and feral, a frenzy of unsated need.

I draw back on a gasp, barely able to break the connection, but I do it because I have to offer. In another life I was a private schoolboy with manners before I found my place in Portland's underbelly. May as well make some use of that trust fund education.

"Tell me I'm not pushing you?" I graze her lips with mine on every damning word.

"I want you to push more," she breathes, her forest green eyes open and locked onto me like she's garnered the corner of my soul and refuses to let go.

Her tongue flicks gently at my bottom lip as she speaks, and my cock is ready to rampage. The quiet touch is intimate, sweet. Erotic. I know instinctively what she'll look like on her knees with her mouth wrapped around my cock.

Addi is a sexy-as-fuck brat, and I want to make it my life's work to tame her, knowing I'll never win, but enjoy the battle nonetheless.

Her lips part as I kiss her slower this time, gliding my tongue along hers, finding how deep she likes it, and when she'll push me away.

Spoiler: she doesn't.

I groan as she climbs me, throwing a denim-clad thigh across my hips until her heat meets my erection. Her breath sharpens against my cheek, but I cup the back of her head, holding her in place so she had no choice but to keep kissing me as she grinds her sinfully hot body against mine.

She reaches between us but I catch her in a grip she can't break. "No, Addi. Not just yet."

She mewls at me and tips her head down to look at me through her lashes. *Brat. Called it.*

"What if I really want to? Or don't you do girls on the first date, K?" She gives me a nickname and my heart pounds like I just scored a touchdown.

"I want to do you right now on the hood of my car." I kiss her again, wanting her lips swollen and flushed as fuck when she has her little meeting with

Mana. "And we will fuck. Soon, I promise. But not just now."

She pouts, wiggling her hips in a figure eight pattern over my groin I swear is designed as an eternal punishment for men alone. "You're turning me down?"

I laugh softly and kiss her hard for a second, only to break back and leave her panting. The pretty pink flush creeps up her cheeks and she stares at me with wild eyes.

"I said soon, Addi." I kiss her hard again, then again, barely able to keep my control in check. "Fuck, you taste good. *Add*ictive."

Her hands claw at my chest. "I want to be closer, Kaleb. Please. Pretty please?" She bats those damn eyelashes at me, linking her arms behind my neck to rub our bodies together. "I want to feel all of you."

"You're doing a damn fine job of that. If this is what burgers do for you, what the hell will it be like when I feed you bacon?"

Her eyes glow when I remember her favorite. "Try me, and find out."

"*Fuckkkk.*"

I tip my head back, desperate for a breath before I do what she's asking me for and fuck her on my car. Her mouth goes to town on my exposed throat, licking and sucking, while her hands pull free of my grip and enter a little downstairs tour below my belt.

She's gentle, folding her small palm around the straining denim at my groin, and squeezing softly. "You do want me," she purrs, while still managing to sound surprised.

"Yeah." My brain is mush. "I want you. I also want to savor every kiss and taste you give me. Take it slow until we're both bursting with need and then that first time together…" I blow out a hard breath as she strokes her fingertips over my cock. "That first time will be fucking unforgettable."

"I want that," she whispers, fitting her body against me and rubbing her breasts to my chest like a kitten in heat. "I want to drip for you."

"Christ, the mouth on you." I fist one hand in her hair, yanking her head back and bow her body so I'm leaning over her, getting right up in her space. My other hand grips over my cock and I fold my fingers around hers. "But if you want to kick-start us off, I like it hard, baby." I squeeze our hands together roughly, crushing her fingers beneath mine.

Her soft "*oooh*," and my labored breaths mingle as I show her how to work me. The combination has me ready to blow in seconds, but I'm determined to edge us both into insanity. Speaking of...

"When you touch yourself tonight, think of me, hell kitten." I kiss her slowly, working her back up and twist our hands so my knuckles rub her denim-encased pussy. "And just as you get close..." I pull our hands away, leaving us both breathless, desperate, and panting. "Stop."

"Huh?" Her eyes flare, wild for a moment, and I nearly come in my pants.

"That right there, kitten, is exactly what I want to see in your face when I fuck you the first time. That edge where you need it so bad, you can't think. That we want each other so much, it's all-consuming."

Her breaths come short. "And if I do get myself off?" Her desperation turns wicked out of necessity.

Denial will be so much fucking fun with her. I smile darkly, reaching out to catch her chin and tap her swollen lips with my thumb. *Perfect.* "I'm not above a funishment date."

"A, um, what?"

I lean closer, wrapping my hand around her throat

and exerting the slightest amount of pressure to show her where we stand. "I can show you pleasure in denial, Addi. In the tiniest addition of pain. And I have a spanking fetish." I smirk, and let her go.

More blood rushes to her lips as she pants for me.

Mission fucking achieved.

I end our date on that little note, easing her into my car with soft promises of more and kissing her gently until that softness resumes, swiping away the desperation I woke in her earlier. There will be time for that later, and later will be soon, because I'm barely in control of myself as it is.

"This was different," Addi murmurs as I start the engine, the familiar purr almost doing as much for me as the girl who was writhing on my lap mere minutes ago.

Almost. But not quite. My obsession with this machine has waned to make room for a new sort that rips through my veins.

"You gonna let me take you out again, Addi?" I sling an arm across the seat back and her shoulders, squeezing her arm, and pull her a little closer.

"Only if there's bacon. And coffee."

I laugh, but beneath her bratty response lies the need awoken in us both that goes well beyond the physical. One date, and I've fallen for this girl like an angel tumbling from grace.

Except I am no angel, and she holds all the grace.

I peel away from our place of solitude, heading back to her house. I leave the window down just enough to flip the bird to the stalkering ass in the trees beyond who watched the whole fucking show from a front row seat.

"You know, I think I will take you out. At least a few more times. Then, you're coming to my place for dinner."

She swallows and leans into my arm slung across her back. "What happens then?"

Then I'll fucking beg you to marry me before someone else does. I clear my throat and mind of the heady image of her in a white dress I get to peel from her body layer by layer and worship her for the next decade and more.

"Then we'll find out if that mouth of yours is as good at kissing other things as it is at sucking my tongue."

That pretty blush of hers lasts the whole trip home.

Am I proud of that last? Damn right I am.

I smirk at the road, and pull her an inch closer. I'll do anything to make sure this girl is mine, and make sure she stays that way.

JADE MARSHALL AND RAVEN HUSH

Chapter Ten

A Line of Sinners

Bowen

I turn away from Kaleb's little make-out session at my hidden position behind the wayward fallen tree with a raging hard-on that shouldn't be possible. I don't like women. Fuck, I don't like anyone. The only reason I get Mana off to the point of agony is because he thinks he deserves punishment, and I fucking well know he does.

The fluids I prefer are the sort black with sin, or red, glistening and running.

Which means there was only one place I could go to get myself off before *Kitten's* little meating with Mana. And meant that way—he'll take his pound of flesh from her one way or the other. Either Kaleb will watch, or he'll join in.

I know his sort. Perfectionist, determined. Thinks his shit doesn't stink like the rest of us. I do, and I fucking well know the stink of sin and the stain an inflated ego leaves on a person's soul. Kaleb will fall, just like the rest of us. And it will be fucking Candyland when he does. Souls like his 'n' hers make a pretty collector's set for a being as powerful as Mana.

I snort as I wind my way into town, to the room beneath the high school where, during daylight hours, the kids play and get their education. Fascist bullshittery, if you ask me, but funnily enough, no one ever does.

No, the gaping hole beneath the school was once a place of ritual where blood was sacrificed across an altar. The place itself holds no power, though the act did. And unbeknownst to the cage-fighting crew who set up there two years prior, they now offer fresh blood in their own sort of ritual.

Same shit, different day.

All one and the same, each sunset running into each other until my existence is all about mother-loving sunshine stained with the tinge of blood. Fuck, I'll coat the place in it if it means I can go home. But I couldn't and I can't, so none of it matters.

Thus, sunrise to sunset, I stalk my newest little obsession, wondering why pretty lips, perky tits, and a cunt I can scent from across town even fucking matter. It shouldn't. *She* shouldn't.

But she does.

My existence's current great mystery, until she ages into dust and I find a new obsession. Something tells me she will keep me going for a millennia or more. Long enough to see Mana's return to the underworld, and I'll be left alone.

Except for maybe Lethe. He's … interesting. Strong, has no idea who or what the fuck he is. But interesting, nonetheless. I wonder if he would like to sample the pleasures of my painful tongue. After all, he is the sort to self-flagellate with a dark joy, just to get up and do it again.

Same shit…

I slink down the stairs, my white, grit-covered clothes stained their usual gray. I'm not above a little mood-based symbolism, but after tonight my clothes will bear a new color, one I won't be able to wash away with a few punches and their saliva that flows across the floor.

Tonight, I intend to end a life and secure my small rein on earth with a little death.

Self-flagellation indeed.

Or perhaps self-sabotage.

Emmanuel's eyes widen when he sees me, his face breaking out into a shaky smile. "Bowen, my friend. What sort of night is it tonight?"

I stare at him, my face blank. That appears to be the thing that scares these mortals the most. Nothingness. Like a psycho ready to kill.

Ah, that's what tonight is, then.

"I'm not your friend. Pick something worthless."

"You mean someone," he mumbles, frowning as he adds my name to the middle of the roster.

I take his pen from his limp, sweaty fingers and cross out all the names. "The first three live. After that…" I shrug. "Who do you want to get rid of?"

His eyes gleam. "I'll make some calls."

I snort in his wake as he hurries the departure from this world of those he hates or who are in his debt that he sees as a liability. Thirteen slots. That's cute. Thirteen favors he will owe me at the end of the night. Not that he understands the depth of his personal depravity right now, but he will.

"*Soon*," I whisper, mocking Kaleb's serenade to his little hellcat. His *kitten*. Excuse me while I puke glowy fucking angel goop on my feet.

The little slut heated up the moment he touched her. Hell, I had God's own trouble keeping my hands out of his, stealing his touches as my own. But breaking them up and causing a fight with Kaleb doesn't suit my plans right now.

And yes, I can say the "G" word without being ended. Well, I was ended, but that was because of a certain incident with another of my kind.

"Cage one. You're good to go," Emmanuel says, all eager like a newborn puppy with his world about to be shattered.

I crack my neck lazily. "All slots taken?"

"Yes. All filled. They'll be arriving…"

Now.

I smirk as a train of men, each lankier or more sinful or just fucking stinkier than the last, parade through the doors. "What did you promise them?"

Emmanuel cackles a little under his breath like a good, ignorant lackey. "Your head with your balls in your mouth."

I smirk. "Creative." Who knew the little slug had it in him?

I pat his shoulder in a familiar, oh-so-human gesture, pressing my fingers along his spine and clicking the bone there. A tiny drop of blood breaks inside his skin, though he doesn't know it yet, and the black mark that stains his flesh as part of our bargain will never disappear. His soul is mine now. Who said it was only up to devils and demons and gods to play such games?

The first three leave the ring quickly. One unconscious, two with many contusions and broken bones. In one of my human facades, I studied medicine back when cadavers were opened on a table beneath many eyes on another continent. When all the modern machines came in, I had to fucking well do it again, both amazed and appalled at how much we got right the first time … and what we didn't.

So many bodies I watched come in and go out. Not all were dead when they arrived, but they left their bodies to meet … well, someone, by the end of the session.

I am no stranger to sin. Much like the multitudes I will claim as my own mini-legion, souls I collect for a battle to come.

The first of the dead men steps into my cage, and I crook my finger.

"Come to Daddy."

I relish the eye roll, the fist that comes my way. At the air that whistles beside my head, the way my jab folds in his windpipe, crushing it. How my elbow at his temple stops him worrying about how to breathe. The touch at the crook of his neck as his soul leaves him and becomes mine.

Nine more to go.

My clothes are drenched with red by the third dead man walking, and when Emmanuel comes in, I smile.

Perhaps it is not just the nothingness expression that terrifies, after all.

It is a good night.

JADE MARSHALL AND RAVEN HUSH

Chapter Eleven

House of Screams

Adreana

I am honestly not looking forward to this bullshit meeting but I know Mana will not let this rest. But he has another thing coming if he thinks he can simply summon me and I'll come running like a damn dog.

Entering Harken in the same outfit I wore for my date, I won't do anything to make him think he has any effect on me. I make a beeline to the bar. A woman with purple hair gazes at me before making her way over.

"You're looking ... different," she says, taking me in.

It takes me a moment to realize she's confusing me with Emma. I should be used to it, she has been my twin my entire life, but it still serves to grate on my nerves.

"You're thinking of my sister," I reply. "I'm Addi."

"Shit," she replies with a blush. "I didn't know."

I wave her off. "You can make it up to me with tequila."

She smiles brightly before grabbing a bottle off the shelf. She twirls it in the air with expertise before pouring a shot and sliding it over to me.

"This one's on me. To make up for putting my foot in my mouth."

Swallowing it down, I slam the little glass on the counter. "Again."

The woman obliges, refilling the glass three more

times before I hold up my hand.

"Damn, girl. Are you trying to get shit-faced or are you readying for battle?"

"More like a war." I grimace before stepping away from the bar. "Do me a favor, though? If you haven't seen me in the next thirty minutes, call the cops. Tell them Mana is a prick and I need saving."

She gapes at me. I don't wait for her to reply before spinning on my heel and making my way through the people who are dancing to an upbeat remix of some kind. From his office window I can see Mana staring down at the throng of people, his gaze locked on me. I know my way through the asylum after all the times I've had to retrieve my sister, so making my way to his office is easy.

I push the door open without knocking, striding in like I own the place. My nerves are shot to shit but there isn't a snowball's chance in hell that I will let Mana see that. His back is still turned to me and I take the moment to assess him. It grates on my nerves that I find him not just attractive, but downright distracting.

His dark dress pants do nothing to hide the fact that this man, this asshole, has a great ass. The black button-up shirt barely contains his muscled back and shoulders. From below the cuffs of his sleeves and the collar of his shirt, black ink peaks out drawing my curious gaze to his exposed flesh.

Fucking Mana.

Grabbing the chair in front of his desk, I relish the loud scraping sound it makes as I drag it back before falling in the soft leather. I must bite back a sigh at the feel against my skin, cool and supple.

"Adreana," Mana says as he turns to face me with a frown. "You're late."

"Not really. I was busy downstairs."

"Yes, shocking and amusing my staff." He sighs as he takes his seat.

"I happen to like your staff. It's you I don't care for."

His eyes flash with irritation. I know he isn't used to being challenged, much less being called out on his bullshit. He glares at me, willing me to give in but I'm not about to bow to any man, much less him.

Although, I might kneel for Kaleb. But now isn't the time for those thoughts.

"Why am I here, Mana? We can't stand each other and rarely talk except to bicker."

He watches me closely, assessing me before speaking.

"We need to discuss your sister's debt."

"The fuck?"

"Don't act dumb, Adreana. We both know she doesn't work here, but parties like there is no tomorrow," he says with a yawn. "Who do you think has been footing her bill?"

"Honestly?" I ask with a raised brow. "I don't give a shit. I'm done with Emma."

Mana tries to hide his surprise but I catch it before he slides his mask back in place.

"That may be, but that doesn't solve my problem. It seems you keep surrounding yourself with people who find themselves indebted to me." The smirk he throws my way is enough to have me grinding my molars to keep from wrapping my hands around his neck.

"I don't know what you expect of me, but I assure you I won't be footing the bill for anyone."

"How was your date?"

The change in conversation leaves me at a loss for words.

"Better than you intended. Lethe was kind enough

to spare us your childish games."

His hands fist on his desk, the only outward sign he offers of the anger brewing inside him. Addi one, Mana zero.

"That's good," he says with a smile that can't be taken as anything but devious. "Did you know your new boyfriend is also in my debt?"

I glare at him, not willing to show my shock or the fact that I feel betrayed. Kaleb swore he would never lie to me. This feels like a lie by omission.

"I said the date went well, not that I was getting married. Kaleb's debt is his business."

"And yet, I'm making it yours."

"What do you want, Mana? Spit it out so I can turn you down and leave. Being here is making my skin crawl."

He chuckles, clearly enjoying my discomfort.

"You can let them die and we both know I've killed for less. Or you can accept my proposal."

Son of a bitch.

Mana watches me as I weigh my options. I may not like my sister but I certainly don't want to see her dead. As for Kaleb? He'll wish he was dead the next time I see him.

"And your offer is…?"

"You're mine. For seven days of my days, no more, no less. If you choose to leave after that, no one will stop you."

Chapter Twelve

Deal with the Devil

Mana

I've played with my little toy long enough. Now it's time she comes to heel. Not that she understands what she's about to agree to, these mortals never do. Nor do they think more than a few moves ahead, and by then...

Her eyes narrow in the sweetest way, like she thinks she can turn me to ash with her hatred. *You know nothing, little mortal.*

"Fine." she grits through her teeth, throwing any remaining caution to the wind. "But my caveat is that you can't threaten either of them again. That's it. That's your freebie."

If only you knew.

"Fine," I echo her sentiment.

"*And,*" she adds, stamping one of her glorious little feet. "I have a deal of my own."

I stare at her, this marvelous little creature come to parlay with the darkest of earthbound gods. "I'm waiting," I murmur, rounding my words with the sort of *come-hither* caress I might use before I lick her from asshole to clit while she creams on my tongue.

"If you kneel for me, you're mine to do with as I wish. For seven of *my* days," the clever little minx answers me, defiance pouring from her in waves, like it's meant to hold me back.

Her efforts fail in epic style. That "fuck you" vibe of hers might as well be an aphrodisiac for all the energy she puts into trying to hold me at bay mentally. Pity, as she doesn't know yet that she'll need it. Soon. Plus, her deal isn't half as damning as mine.

"Done," I say blithely, slapping my palm to the desktop with a hard crack. My whip leaps from the desk and I flick it aside for the moment.

She jumps, cute as she is, but that last wasn't for her.

Bowen appears out of thin air at my side, bowing with false platitudes and covered in blood. Maybe some other things.

"What the—" she starts.

I wave her to silence. "What are you wearing?" I frown at the ruined angel. Gore and guts drip from his saturated clothes like he's been bathing in mortal blood. "What did you do, Bowen?" My voice holds a hard edge, because my pretty little torment isn't playing by the rules.

"I had … fun." He licks his lips, tasting the blood of others, and smiles.

Something in me rises and for the moment it's not my cock. My demon scents him, his sin, and I need *more.*

We all act as though we rule this plane when in fact it defines us. And we all sure as hell want to go home. Each of us will do anything to achieve that. But what Bowen's done…

"You know you can't go back now," I whisper, cradling his face between my hands, slicking my thumbs in the residual life force of those he tore apart. "Yours is a one-way trip, my friend."

He blinks at me, all sultry and sinuous as his damp body plasters to mine. "Perhaps I only want to go down, Master," he whispers, rising on his toes to press his lips to my mouth.

I let him kiss me, allowing his flickering tongue with its oh-so-sinful offering to tempt me. He sucks my tongue as Adreana watches, silent for the moment. My eyes remain open while the twisted fallen debases himself further, groveling for my kisses, but I only have a place for her at my side. Never him, though he doesn't seem to have worked that out yet.

She is who and what I crave and the only person who knows I own her in her entirety right now is *me*. That little juicy secret hardens me and I know it's time to claim her, in my own way.

I cup the back of Bowen's neck, flicking my tongue along his until he whimpers, and reach down to squeeze his balls through his blood-stained leather pants. "I want you to do something for me," I purr, giving him *fuck me* eyes. Which I'll deliver on. It just won't be what he wants. I swallow a laugh. My deals never are.

"Anything," he promises me.

"Good," I growl. "Now be a good penitent and be my vessel."

The whites of his eyes show as I use my hand on his nape to push him forward over my desk. Things tumble off the sides as I hold him down, though he struggles prettily for me.

I smile. "Take notes," I murmur to Addi. This conversation will be between us, now.

"But, I—" Bowen starts.

"Shhh." I place a comforting finger over his lips that seals nicely for me until I'm done.

The angel weeps on my desk, blood and sweat collecting in a small pool that I make sure to rub his face into. He might cry now but if I reach between his legs, I know I'll find him hard as hell at the humiliation. The sick little fuck gets off on the shit I throw his way, and we both love it.

"You're insane." Addi backs away, but I shake my head.

"Stay."

Her feet freeze in place as she starts to understand the mere edges of my power. Her lips move, but for once nothing comes out, and I'm not even the one doing that.

"Welcome to my world, little mortal," I breathe.

She pants, her eyes darting to the writhing angel beneath me who just appeared out of thin air, and back to my face. "I didn't know—"

"And now you do," I whisper, still smiling faintly. "I'll claim you now, Adreana. Desk, or chair?" I gesture to the plush leather recliner in one corner away from my desk. I'm not above offering comfort while I violate her. That's not the sort of monster I am. There's a simple pleasure in being kind as well as cruel, but the power comes in hope.

When she scurries for the corner of my room without question this time, clambering aboard, I sigh at the sweet taste that flicker leaves behind. Like if she's allowed to curl there, she'll remain unmolested.

Interesting that she doesn't try to fight for the innocence of the angel beneath me, but then, he looks like a monster in his own way too, as much as he is becoming. I appreciate the beauty around me, at its best, before I ruin it forever.

"Relax," I murmur to both of them. "It's easier that way."

Bowen humps my desk pitifully while Addi frowns.

"What…"

I send out a flicker of power, reaching into my reserves. Later I'll have to give my essence to the Chemist, but for now, I can play.

Claws burst from the arms of the chair and its tall back, one silencing her before the first scream leaves her throat. The others grip a wrist each, clamping them down. The fourth … I let that wander her stomach, systematically shredding her shirt until her chest is bared to me.

Frightened eyes watch me over cascading tears as she sobs. Then the hand clamps over her tit, rolling the nipple teasingly between razored tips and a new awareness that scares her worse enters those green eyes: need.

I laugh at her as I rip Bowen's pants down to free his balls and his asshole to the air. I won't be needing the rest tonight and neither will he. I place my hand on his bare ass.

"Remember, Bowen. My vessel." He'll feel my body tearing into his, but there will be no pleasure for him tonight. Not unless it's the painful sort, though he likes that, too.

Recompense for puncturing my balls after our torturous playtime the other night. He nods and rests his cheek on my desk, the fight leaving him.

"Good little fallen," I coo.

Addi's eyes widen, and she does try to scream behind the hand that covers her mouth. One of mine, in my demon form, but she's not ready for that yet. She's not ready for any part of me, but tonight she will take my phantom as I ruin her hole by hole.

"Uff oooo!" Her muffled defiance reaches me in a stream of heady pleasure.

"Oh, I will." I lock eyes with her and stroke Bowen asshole to balls and back again.

Her wriggling stops. Those green eyes flick down, then back to me.

"Mana?" she mumbles, snorting her panic through her nose.

"Relax," I whisper, spitting onto Bowen's asshole and pushing my finger against it.

His sphincter gives way, because we've been here

before. Her little virgin ass? That I'd tear. But here, a flush fills her face and breasts with a delicious pink tinge I want to lick from her skin as I finger her ass by proxy.

Bowen's hole squeezes down tight, but I don't berate him. He's being a good vessel and letting me feel what she feels. Her already bearing down on me tells me she's in need of a good dozen anal orgasms.

I sink my finger deeper and add a second, offering them no mercy as I stretch the hole before me. I let the claw manifested on her chair that's an extension of myself drop from her mouth to close gently around her throat, holding her up and reminding her who owns her now.

Those pretty ruby lips are parted and the demon in me wants to paint them in the sin that will soon fill her insides. She whimpers so prettily as I ease my fingers from the flesh before me. I rub my crotch as she watches, hardening myself to the point of bursting before I push my pants aside and press the tip of my cock to Bowen's sacrificial asshole.

And what a sacrifice it will be.

He groans low in his throat as I push inside, accommodating me as he has done many times before. That makes him perfect for the job of violating my newest toy without tearing her apart. Him, however...

I watch the drop of blood that trails down the back of his pale thigh to add to the stain on his pants. His chest heaves with taking me, and I break the hypnotic rhythm to fix my attention on Addi.

Her legs tremble, her fists clench, and her mouth is open in a perfect "O" shape to accommodate my cock. The cock that might kill her if I touch her with it.

My loss, her gain, perhaps. If I'm an insufferable torment now, I can only imagine what I'll be like if I sink flesh deep into her body without searing her insides and ending her mortal life on the spot. Her innocence is a mark I can't remove. That's not my choice.

I won't kill her as she's my favorite thing.

My hips work gently as I push my length into the angel. The little ring stretches nicely, and I trace a finger around him, humming my moan as I sink into her body, filling her while she writhes on nothing but air.

"Mana—" Her whisper reaches me faintly as her eyes roll in her head.

"Not yet." I slap Bowen's ass, and she cries out. My smile lets my fangs out and I show them to her, unashamed as she panics harder, her ass clenching down on my phantom cock. "Hold on, little toy of mine." I ram my full length into the angel beneath me, his body rippling with the violence of my action.

Addi's mouth hangs open in a scream only a true angel can hear. Pity we don't have one about to test my theory on. The ruined one below me humps back, part his own motion, but there's some of her in that. I moan my satisfaction, driving myself knot-deep into the open hole and settle my weight over him.

"Hold on now," I whisper, fixated on the trembling, moaning, and sobbing girl across the room.

My foreskin peels back, freeing my two cocks, their tongue-like forms stroking and weaving in her ass, like entities with their own minds. I don't need to move as they fuck her for me now, each pulsing and plunging ever deeper, seeking the sin in her and absorbing that into me, strengthening me. Not that she has a lot to feed on but— There. Self satisfaction. My little toy likes to get herself off, stealing away her pleasure from the world.

Not anymore. Her pleasure is mine, and only myself and those I allow to torment her in turn will enjoy her stolen sin.

She cries out, her legs opening. The claws holding

her wrists release to tear her jeans from her body, leaving the scrap of lace she calls underwear, exposing a growing wet spot as she gushes for me. But I know she hasn't come for me yet. That's my next agenda.

I reach between myself and the angel and tickle his balls. "Up, boy," I mock him.

Bowen rises on shaking arms, bracing himself as I reach lower and find his cock. Perhaps I have a use for that after all. Freeing him, I clench his cock in my fist, strangling him until his body convulses, nearing his edge. Pain gets this sick fuck off, just like it does Kaleb, though I doubt he knows that part of himself. Yet. My thumb caresses the drop of pre-cum at the tip of Bowen's cock, and he snorts through his nose, fighting me every second.

I press my lips to his ear, still watching Addi. "I need her to come and come and come, and you are my vessel, angel. So, you will also come and come until it hurts so bad it ruins your immortal soul forever." It won't, but he needs the words to get himself off.

My thumb rubs his cock like it's her clit and that's exactly what Addi feels. Her legs spread wider and her haunting cry circles the room as her body pulses.

Bowen disgraces himself on my hand as I smile at her, licking my fangs.

"Good girl," I coo as she settles from her first orgasm, her ass clenching down on my cocks. They go wild inside her, driving her back to the edge too fast. Her breathless cry is more pain than pleasure now, and she's perfect. "Shall we go again?"

She shatters almost instantly, my little sinner, and I jolt my hips a few times just to bury my knot deeper. She won't take that, but Bowen will, soon. After a few more. We're almost through my quota when the door to my office is thrown open.

Kaleb stalks in, murder in his eyes. It's a damn

good look on him.

"The fuck are you doing? You said—"

"I said you could take her out. But now I own her, forever," I add silkily, purely for the perverse pleasure of watching her eyes bulge, though his horror is greater than hers.

"You did *what?*" he hisses in a low voice that makes my cocks twine together.

I fuck her ass harder, bringing her back to the edge and holding her there while Kaleb stupidly tries to negotiate with me.

"I own her. My deal."

The air stills in my office. Kaleb strains against an invisible force—his conscience perhaps—and tries not to launch at me. I flick my whip at him, and he catches the end. Our tug-of-war doesn't end until he pulls it free of my hand—or I let go, whichever thought he chooses to believe. What interests me is that he can touch my whip and not be burned.

"Seven days," she whispers, breaking the pervading silence.

"Seven of my days," I correct her. "Fuck, you're more beautiful than ever, taking me."

Kaleb swivels to see her—really see her—for the first time, and his entire body shakes. "What did you agree to, Addi?" he whispers, tracing her lips as she comes again, shuddering and gazing at him through lust-glazed eyes. "Fuck, I wanted you so bad." His voice cracks on that last and I give in an inch.

Part of an inch.

"Do you know how long seven days are in hell, little mortal?" I breathe. "Eternity has no limit and every minute is drawn out. I can play with you like this forever, tear you apart and put you back the way I want, and tomorrow—every tomorrow—you will still be mine."

Her sobs stop as she stares at me. A shudder runs through her as her ass contracts on my cocks and she comes without my help.

I grit my teeth at the deluge of pleasure she torments me with. Her body creates a chain reaction I can't prevent. I fill my knot, sending stream after stream of filth and sin into her body while Bowen wears my pain. He ejaculates on my hand that still clenches on his length, dirtying us and disgracing us both further.

"Fuck," I gasp, still staring at her. I have a mind to make her lick up the mess she just created.

My little toy came so hard she took us all with her, just at the mention of being tied to me for eternity. A forever full of torment.

Isn't that interesting?

I smile at Kaleb as my knot lessens a tiny bit, savoring the shock on his face, devouring her pain and pleasure and the haunted, needy look in her eyes. Hells below, she'll be on her knees well before me, licking my shoes and anything else I want to use to occupy that glorious, cocks-worthy mouth.

Finally, I slip free of my vessel's hole and tuck myself away. My legs wobble as I stride with a confidence I don't feel around my desk, tapping Bowen's mouth to free him. The angel gasps weakly, and slides to the floor.

The hands holding Addi release her. She sighs, her body softening, and she smiles—my toy fucking *smiles* at me.

Kaleb takes her into his arms, glaring at me as my sins trickle from where they stain her insides. Slowly, he kneels, lowering them both to the thick carpet of my office.

I crouch beside them and touch her face tenderly. "You're mine, now, Adreana. In every way. But I promise I'll let Kaleb share you in my down times. He can have you right now, if he cleans you up."

Kaleb's brows knit as he nods at me, an astute level of caution in his eyes.

It should be there.

"All right…" He cups her face and strokes her cheek as she softens in his arms, drifting to sleep.

It's beautiful to watch and haunting, and I feel empty all at once, needing always that which I can't have.

"Clean my cum from her ass with your tongue if you want the privilege of sharing her," I add delicately and step over them, heading to the dungeon for my own version of torture. The secret of Kaleb's existence can wait a while longer.

He groans as I leave, and a glance over my shoulder at the doorway which provides the perfect view of him between her legs, his tongue extended to soothe her tortured little asshole, swallowing my cum. The torment he'll put up with to have her. My smile is back as I walk to my own penance.

I can't have my toys having all the fun, after all.

JADE MARSHALL AND RAVEN HUSH

Chapter Thirteen

Their Penance, and Mine

Adreana

What in the ever-loving fuck have I gotten myself into? The thought plays through my mind on a constant loop as pleasure assaults me from everywhere. I watch Mana accost the blood-covered man whose name I can't remember. In moments it seems like he is in pain but a split-second later he seems blissed out.

I don't understand what the hell is going on but what I do know is I have never experienced pleasure like this in my entire short life. For a moment, I forget the insanity of the entire situation. I now understand why my sister is so very eager to fall at Mana's feet every chance she gets. He hasn't even touched me, though I still feel the *invasion* of him within me, and I can admit to myself I am already addicted.

I want to beg him to stop but I want to continue this pleasure-filled ride for the rest of my life.

It takes a moment for my mind to catch up to what is happening around me, my focus solely on Mana and the phantom cocks—yes, more than one, I am sure of it—he has buried inside me. I have never been fucked in the ass, fear of the pain always holding me back, but if this is anal sex, then sign me up.

Mana speaks, but I don't hear his words. They aren't meant for me. Turning my head, I see Kaleb standing in the doorway, visibly shaking as he tries to contain his rage.

"You did *what*?" he hisses in a low voice that

raises goose bumps along my arms.

Why is he so angry? It's just sex. And after my time is done, both he and Emma will be free of Mana. I'm doing this to protect them.

My thoughts shatter as Mana's cocks fuck me harder even though I fight to keep up with the conversation. I need to know what the fuck is going on.

"I own her. My deal."

The look on Mana's face is one of pure bliss but it has nothing to do with the sex. No, it's dark pride in being able to one-up Kaleb. I want to roar in outrage. I would have kept this from him, never let him know the sacrifice I have made to keep him and my sister safe.

It may sound naive but I feel like Kaleb is part of something bigger. That he was brought into my life for more than just a little fun. He speaks to my soul, and he makes me happy. I don't want to lose that.

"Seven days," I whisper, breaking the tension between the two of them.

"Seven of my days," Mana amends. "Fuck, you're more beautiful than ever, taking me."

Kaleb's gaze finds me for the first time and I wish he didn't have to see this. I watch the frown line on his forehead deepen as his gaze darkens. I don't know what it looks like to him but I feel exposed. I know I'm spread out like a whore. My cunt dripping, begging to be filled while my ass is gloriously violated. Mana's cocks twitch inside me and I can't hold back the shudder that works its way through me.

Kaleb approaches, his hand cupping my cheek, his teeth sinking into his bottom lip as he takes in my disheveled, sweat-drenched form. My breasts heave, my nipples distended, begging for any form of attention. The words sit on the tip of my tongue, ready to beg Kaleb to do something, anything.

"What did you agree to, Addi?" he whispers, tracing my lips with his fingertip as I come again, shuddering, and gazing at him through hooded eyes. "Fuck, I wanted you so bad." His voice cracks on that last and my heart stutters in my chest.

Doesn't he want me anymore? I knew in my heart this may be too much for him to handle but I was hoping he would understand.

"Do you know how long seven days are in hell, little mortal?" Mana asks, cutting in, still buried balls-deep in the man he has trapped across the surface of his desk. "Eternity has no limit and every minute is drawn out. I can play with you like this forever, tear you apart and put you back the way I want, and tomorrow—every tomorrow—you will still be mine."

My orgasm pulls me beneath the surface, drowning out all sight and sound. Why the fuck does being bound to Mana for an eternity make my stomach flip over and my soul beg for more? That can't be right. I'm not even sure what the fuck he is and suddenly I want to spend every moment in his dark embrace?

No. Mana is evil. Of that, I am sure. He is using my own body against me, trying to force me into things I don't want. If only that was true. Lying to myself won't do a damn thing about the situation I find myself in.

My body is cradled in strong arms when I finally come down from the high of my last orgasm. Opening my eyes, I see Kaleb's face, fear and longing scrolled across his features. I want to reach out and touch him, say something to assure him I still want to be his, but I don't get the opportunity.

Mana leans in, cupping my face and I nuzzle—yes, I fucking nuzzle—deeper into his touch. "You're mine, now, Adreana. In every way," he says. "But I promise I'll let Kaleb share you in my down times. He can have you right now, if he cleans you up."

The self-satisfied smirk that crosses his features is enough to make me want to slap him. I hold back, though, wanting to know if I can still keep Kaleb.

"All right…" Kaleb murmurs, touching my face.

I feel sleep trying to pull me into the darkness and I try to fight it.

"Clean my cum from her ass with your tongue if you want the privilege of sharing her," Mana adds before silence descends.

Cold wood presses against my back as Kaleb lays my spent form down. I assume I am placed on Mana's desk. My thighs are pressed open and I should say something. I should protest what is about to happen. But I can't find the words or the will to do even that.

"You belong to him now," Kaleb whispers in my ear, his palm lightly caressing my left breast. "But I won't give you up, Addi. I'll take whatever I can get."

His lips skim along my neck, over my breasts and stomach to stop above my pubic bone. Kaleb's breathing is harsh, puffs of wind hitting my oversensitized clit. His tongue touches the ring of my ass sending shudders through my entire body.

Kaleb takes this as encouragement, lapping at whatever it is currently leaking out of me. The feel of his lips on me, the taboo notion of him cleaning up another man's cum, has a loud moan falling from my lips.

"Kaleb," I moan brokenly as he feasts on me.

Two thick fingers press inside my pussy and I can't help but bow off the wood beneath me. I haven't even recovered from the onslaught that Mana delivered and already my body is begging for more.

Kaleb's lips make their way higher between my thighs until he has my clit sucked into his mouth, harshly sucking while relentlessly flicking with his tongue.

"May I?" a voice asks beside my head.

I didn't realize the other man was still in the office. I want to refuse, not sure I can handle much more, but the way he stares at me has me nodding. Never in my wildest dreams would I have imagined all these men to be interested in me.

Deep down I know this may just be about sex. But I have lived a life full of restraint, always doing the right thing. In this moment, I am simply doing what I want. I will deal with the consequences in the morning.

Lips lock around one of my nipples and another broken cry falls from my lips. It feels like the torture has been going for hours. Teeth clamp down on the distended nub and I can't hold back the orgasm that follows. Nonsense words tumble forth from deep within me, tainting the air around us.

A cock notches at my entrance as tears fall down my face. It's all too little and too much at the same time. I want to beg Kaleb to fuck me until I beg him to stop, but I don't know how much more I can handle. My body is spent, my ass is ruined, and I know if I come one more time I will definitely pass out.

"You belong to me as well," Kaleb groans as he feeds me inch after inch of his thick cock.

I try to bring my body upright but a large hand keeps me in place. My nipple releases with a pop before those same lips suck on my earlobe.

"I have always wanted to see him like this," the man whispers. "Kaleb is a stunning man, his cock even more so. Seven inches of thick, veiny, delicious dick."

Kaleb thrusts harshly into me, his anger at the situation bleeding through now that he's let go. Hands fondle my breasts roughly, the pain pushing me closer to the edge as the man continues to whisper in my ear.

"I wish I was you," he murmurs. "I would fall to

feel this man fuck me. To lose himself in me as he does with you."

My eyes connect with his, sadness swimming in his gaze.

"How did Mana do it?" I whisper.

I suddenly feel this urgency to help this broken creature, to give him what he wants. He stares at me for the longest moment before taking my hand in his. He presses my index and middle finger together before raising them to his lips.

It's instant, the moment we are connected. I can feel everything he feels and by the look on his face I assume it goes both ways. All my senses are heightened, every nerve ending in my body firing on all cylinders.

The man howls out in pleasure while Kaleb curses.

"What the fuck did you do, Bowen?" he rasps.

"Nothing she didn't want," he replies with a smile. "I told you I would have you eventually."

Kaleb's movements are still as he glares at Bowen and I want to cry.

"Move," I beg brokenly.

"Addi, you don't know…" Kaleb starts but I cut him off.

"Fuck me," I demand angrily. "Or find me someone who will."

Anger slashes across his features as he throws my leg over his shoulder.

"I'll fuck you," he rages, punctuating each word with a brutal thrust. "You won't even remember another man by the time I'm through with you."

The sound of a zipper draws my attention. Watching Bowen's shaking hand as he struggles to free his erection is strangely erotic. To know that whatever is happening here affects him so much has a smile stretching across my face.

Kaleb hammers into me, my breasts bouncing wildly as my orgasm approaches at a rapid speed. I push Bowen's hands aside, wrapping my own around his length, bringing him half onto the wooden surface of the table.

Everything is a blur. It's dirty and forbidden, the noises are animalistic and beautiful. Kaleb's thrusts start to lose their tempo right before he pulls out of me. His cock head slaps against my clit three times before jets of white cum land on my stomach. Bowen's cock kicks in my hand and paints my breasts in a similar fashion.

The obscenity of the situation sends me over the edge, screaming.

And then I black out.

Chapter Fourteen

Break and Enter

Lethe

The walls inside Sinner's End fold around me in an embrace made of pure sin. I can scent the damage done inside the very air of this place. If Harken is a hellspawn's playground, then the girl who holds Mana's current obsession's house is Oregon's version of original sin.

Whatever the hell happened in this place, I don't want to be any part of it, and yet I'm drawn here, like the pores of this place call to me.

Or the creature who resides within.

Adreana.

I don't understand the deep craving my fragmented soul needs any more than I understand my purpose in this place, in this world. A flicker of life is all that drives me in a singular direction. Mana has his torments. Bowen his murders. Even Kaleb has a defined existence, while I suffer through a haze, here one second and floating the next.

I woke up this morning inside Sinner's End with no more memory of why I am here or how I made my way inside the house. Or any answers to any of the questions. Only more questions. Never-ending, tormenting questions.

One day I want to know what sleep feels like. That hasn't happened for me yet either. For now, I trail my fingers along these tainted walls and breathe in the air I share with my obsession. One I share with all of them—

Mana, Bowen, Kaleb. We all want her. And she will ruin us all.

I watched Mana limp down the hall to the basement where he pays his penance, already drawn and aged at the thought of the chair his Chemist binds him to. I wonder if either of them knows who is in control, or if either of them cares for more than the simple end result.

And yet, here she is, in the place where I find myself wandering empty halls like a ravenous phantom with one destination: her.

Kaleb took her home from the asylum once he and Bowen finished playing with her. I watched them leave, but my feet took me instead to Mana, where I stood behind his chair as he deflated like a discarded toy, no longer in use. Or perhaps simply all used up.

I find the stairs, gliding silently along them until I arrive at a pair of bedroom doors. One is empty, the sister she's tried to remove from her life. That won't last, but I don't understand how I know that little skerrick of information.

Adreana sleeps peacefully, her tired body draped across her bed, washed, and clothed in a pale cotton nightgown that hides just enough of her perfect flesh to be painfully tantalizing. Kaleb must have done that, and a twinge of irritation slithers along my spine at the mortal's intervention. That he has touched her, marked, and claimed her burns my insides brutally. The desire to singe his flesh to ash while she watches sweeps over me, and I push the darkest thoughts away. *This place is pure evil.*

How she could reside within and not be tainted, I don't understand, either. My innocence—no, my *ignorance*—cripples me as I kneel by her bed and curve my palm around the shape of her face, without touching her. Heat warms my palm, her soft, dark lashes fluttering with the disturbance of her room. But if she's going to wake…

I may as well cave to my obsession as the others have to theirs. It's not like I am a perfect man, and giving in to her seems the perfect answer to my plight.

My fingertips brush her skin. A faint, pink blush warms her flesh beneath my touch. The color spreads, curving beneath her eyes and traveling down her neck to the tops of her breasts. A flick of the thin, cotton strap leaves her exposed to me. I suck in a long breath, willing myself to remain in control, but she's so beautiful. So fucking beautiful lying there, her body reacting to me even though she doesn't know I'm here. My cock thickens inside my pants and I swallow back the urge to free myself and desecrate her pretty skin, leaving her bound in my silken ropes.

She shivers in her sleep, one hand drifting across her chest to brush my wrist. Her fingers leave a burning path with each caress, as though she acknowledges my presence. Those slim, pale hands curl around my wrist, holding gently, and she lets out the softest sigh that leaves my blood sizzling in my veins.

My thumb presses against her lips where they part slightly, the tip of her tongue gliding over my skin. I suck in a sharp breath. *Is this why I'm here? To defile her, and myself?* Temptation never bothered me in the short history of my remembered existence, but I do know she's made for me, and that I belong to her. Like a possession? Mana would have a field day with that, a demon's delight, but I don't care.

I press my thumb deeper, parting her lips a little wider. She lets me, rolling to one side and leaning into my touch, the very tip of her tongue testing my flesh with tiny strokes. I groan, fisting my cock through my pants with my other hand, but it's too much. Being here, with her … I'll shatter for her, fragment into a thousand pieces for this mortal who holds me enthralled.

Reaching into my pants I grip my cock tight and thumb the head. I've never let anyone touch me, willingly, or take part in Mana's impromptu orgies, preferring to watch and suffer, but this moment is one where I cross a personal line when I rest the head of my cock to her lips and she sucks me in.

Blood rushes south, leaving me rocking on my knees at her bedside as she sucks the tip of my cock like it's her personal pacifier. I let out a soft groan, unable to keep my need in, my craving too great within the warm, wet confines of her pretty mouth that's the perfect shape for me.

"I'm yours, Addi," I murmur, knowing I won't last more than a handful of seconds.

My prediction comes true as she sucks oh-so-softly on my cock, and I plunge to the back of her throat, coating her in my silk. A shuddered breath leaves her as I pull out, glossing her lips gently with my cum, defiling her beautifully.

I tuck myself back in, my hands shaking as I rest my lips against her temple.

"All yours," I promise her sleeping form, and thumb the pearlescent drop at the corner of her lips back into her mouth. She sucks just as gently and I harden impossibly, aching inside and out.

My steps take me unconsciously back to the open window, and I lean out of it, knowing the fall won't kill me when I land on the hallowed ground of the cemetery that butts up against the house. Its borders include Sinner's End, Addi's house within the glowing blue circle that encompasses the graveyard, creating an end to the city's limits, a place I know Mana cannot cross.

I don't understand the knowledge or its origins, but I lean into the night air and nearly scream at the red-

and-white splattered horror that floats outside her window.

My drop to the ground is less than graceful. I manage to land in a crouch, stumbling only for a second before I find my feet.

"What are you doing here?" I ask the horror that floats gently to my side.

"Watching her, like you," Bowen mocks me, his too-pale eyes glittering in his pigmentless face. "Except tonight you took more than you gave, didn't you, little innocent?"

My cock strains at the thought of her sleeping form, her lips wrapped around me, sucking me off. "Not so innocent," I murmur, letting the destroyed soul walk at my side.

"No," he says, shaking his head. "So, I wonder, what does that make you now?"

"I know not what I was or what I became," I quote the words like they were ingrained into me in some past life.

Bowen chuckles softly, stepping out onto the short, arched bridge that crosses the stream at the edge of Sinner's End's land. "Oh, yes. The words of your maker etched on your soul. Let's fall together, shall we?"

He mounts the edge of the bridge, his arms open wide like a sacrifice, and topples backward. I frown, but there's no splash and when I glance over the edge, the water beneath is undisturbed.

Bowen is gone and despite his strange invitation, I walk silently across the town to Harken, reaching the asylum's shadows just as the sun breaks the horizon, lighting everything with its too-bright rays not made for a creature that slinks in the shadows. Before its light can reach me, I'm safely ensconced within Harken's walls along with all the other broken, tortured souls.

JADE MARSHALL AND RAVEN HUSH

The ones just like me.

Chapter Fifteen

Drink to Obsession

Mana

My world is filled with creepers. Like that blank-faced angel who doesn't remember the last millennia of his existence yet follows me downstairs to watch my daily demise. The same demented creature who holds my metaphorical fucking hand like a perfect nursemaid.

Hell, by the time the Chemist is done sucking my veins dry like a clinical vampire, I don't remember my own name. Lethe sits with me while I return to the world, though it must have taken a handful of hours. His eyes trace the syringes that permeate my skin like a freakish hedgehog, lining my ribs and stomach, tracing my outline in a monstrous fashion.

The Chemist is my designer, me his creation. He walks around me, tweaking and hissing when the venom in my veins fills tube after tube, each paler than the next. Until my usefulness wanes. A fog hangs over me, weighing me down as I sink in the chair he tethers me to, with leather straps that dig into the skin of an old man.

I remain in that state, wrinkled and used up, until he removes the needles, letting my blood drip onto the bare, cracked cement floor. My mortal life ebbs away with blood that refills my depleted meat sack of a form until my legs shake when I try to rise. The Chemist's fingers trace over the leather bands that hold me in place, knowing I have no strength left to fight him.

A stolen glance at the angel seated at my feet by that point leaves me wondering if he intends to leave me in the chair for another round against my will.

Free will. The greatest joke of mortal existence.

Lethe remains, though he reaches out at one point to touch my leg. Offer reassurance, perhaps, that I didn't die and was reborn alone? A gargled objection from me and the offer is retracted, though he remains, still and silent, a sentinel in the underbelly of this heinous place. Neither of us speaks or acknowledges the other until I attempt to rise, and fucking fall on my demon-spawned ass.

Then Lethe reaches out a hand, one I batted away and pretended didn't sting me with the touch of his pristine skin. Not that he'd remain so unscathed if he resided at Harken, or anywhere near her.

"*Don't touch me, choir boy,*" I spit, swiping claws at him.

The sinless fucker simply leans out of my way and watches me climb the stairs, boring twin holes into the back of my head. The pressure releases as I reach the ground floor, emerging from the space beneath the asylum, and I know he's gone.

No bonus points for guessing where my little angel might go, as he leaves the asylum every night. He thinks he's sneaky, or perhaps he has no control over the urge. That measure of obsession is something I understand intimately.

The club is alive when I force myself to set foot on the main floor, letting those craving an easy death, or a night of forgotten sin touch me like I'm their inverse Messiah. My lips turn up as I feed off their desires, their twisted needs, some so dark they barely acknowledge them inside the silence of their own minds.

And with my drug circulating the floor and the mezzanine balcony above, how silent the cacophonous crowd is. Screaming on the outside, and dead within.

More than one face as blank as Lethe's turns my way, hands reaching, drawn to their deliverer. As though some part of each of their vacant minds recognizes the mercy I offer their burning, worthless souls.

A mercy I might call to collect on in future, should I have a need of an army who crave my attention, a secret lodged within the deepest, most shadowy part of their hearts.

Breaking through the crowd, I slide behind the bar, tapping Kaleb's replacement on the shoulder and claiming a bottle of tequila. If I'm going to forget fucking Adreana the way I plan with no true contact to her blemishless skin, I will earn a mortal level hangover to go alongside it in the morning.

It seems self-sabotage is the order of the day—or night, as it were.

"Are you going to claim her as yours in front of all of them?" Kaleb appears at my shoulder like the fucking wraith of a hellspawn he is.

"Creepy fuck," I grunt. The fucking place is full of them. "You finish her like a good little pet?"

"Do you mean did I finish *in* her?" he snaps back and sluices a hand through his wet hair, spraying droplets of water scented like her across my face. "No. I fucking painted her with my lust, nearly tore her with my fury, took her home, cleaned her up, and tucked her into bed with a good-night kiss."

"And then you'll beg for her forgiveness like you can take it all back and be her date again," I mock him, not looking at the man in case I end him on the spot.

He still thinks he's mortal. I know better.

"Unlike you, I can offer her a life. A real one," he says quietly in that way of his designed to convict me of my sins.

I laugh in his face. "You can try, hellspawn. But

that girl has more claims on her than you know."

"No one else fucking well touches her," he snarls at me, spitting in my face.

I let his spittle drip along my cheek before I swipe the liquid off and clean my fingers gently against his shoulder, stepping into his space until we share a heady breath. "There's a force at play you don't understand, child," I murmur, tracing the curve of his cheek with my fingertips. "You can't take her from her fate, and you can't save her. Only follow, if that's what she'll allow. For any of us," I muse in the silence between songs before the club is relit in a strobing black light and a beat that shifts the foundations and the souls captured in these hideous walls. "Did you fuck her alone?"

His teeth bare. "No."

I nod, understanding. "Bowen?"

"Fuck you," he hisses, his jaw clenched. Tendons stand out on the man's neck, their sharp silhouette mangled with the twisted inked fingers that wind along his throat.

"I warned you, but you didn't listen. She is ours."

"*She* gets her own choice." The white devil appears between us.

Kaleb jerks back. "Fucker."

"Indeed." Bowen smiles, a dead thing that rattles these mortal bones. "I believe your friend downstairs needs more. It's not enough." His facade drops and he frowns. "Would you like me to source a replacement?" His gaze wanders over me and for a moment I wonder if he cares, or if there's something bigger at play here.

My warning of a moment before to Kaleb rebounds against me and I deflect the angel's quiet inquisition. *I'll find your game. Then I'll use it to destroy you.*

I enjoy the fervor of a twisted, stained soul as

much as the next demon, but Bowen is something else entirely. With the addition of Lethe to our obsessed little circle jerk, I can't see the end game, and that fucks with my night.

I give Kaleb a sharp nod. "You're on daylight duty, baby boy. I'll be … occupied for a while."

"Like a flaccid goon bag," Bowen adds with a crooked smile that shows the angel's fangs.

Fuck knows why they need them, but I'd never met an angel without a ferocious pair.

"Good night, sleep tight," Bowen sings over the club's music.

Many of the blank faces turned to face us, and for a moment, in the frozen strobe light, their eyes glow a lurid green. A pressure builds in my chest, my skin ice on my bones.

Music returns along with sound as Kaleb frowns at me, his mouth opening, but I don't want his concern.

Tonight is more fucked than any other night.

I should be celebrating at the way I defiled Adreana, but some part of me acknowledges Kaleb might have it right.

I want to kneel and beg her forgiveness, earn her pretty kisses and her soft hands on my face, read the adoration and love in her eyes.

Fuck me as a grandstanding fool.

I storm from the main floor, heading down the retched steps to let the Chemist torture me a little more as Adreana works her way deeper into my blood, changing me one demon-sludge-filled pint at a time.

JADE MARSHALL AND RAVEN HUSH

Chapter Sixteen

A Demon's Playground

Adreana

I dream of Mana.
I dream of Kaleb.
I dream of hands, and tongues, and cocks. Pushing, pulling, pinching, thrusting, fucking.

I wake up in a state of arousal I am most definitely not acquainted with, and I swear I can taste cum on my tongue.

But that isn't possible. Of all the things I did and allowed yesterday, that was not part of it. I contemplate getting up to brush my teeth but settle for pulling my vibrator from my drawer. I can't stand feeling all pent up and frustrated. Which I shouldn't really, not after the way I was used in Harken just last night. But I am, and there it is.

I turn the unit to its highest setting and thrust it inside my dripping hole. Are there still bodily fluids spilling from inside me or am I just that horny? The moment the vibrations hit inside me, a scream tears from my lungs as I gush all over my bed. The orgasm is unexpected and feels like it drags on for hours. The muscles in my back and thighs hurt from holding me off the mattress.

The thing that disturbs me most and has tears spilling down my cheeks is the voice on loop in my head. Mana.

Beg me.
You know you want it.

Feel me.

****

I passed out after the orgasm finally released me from its grip, my body simply too spent to continue. I feel the vibration against my leg and realize I never even switched off my toy before succumbing to the darkness.

"Did I not do a good enough job last night?"

The voice in the corner of my room has a different kind of scream choking up my throat.

"Fucking asshole!" I yell, throwing my bedside lamp at Kaleb's head.

He ducks without care, his gaze never leaving my form. His eyes darken before I realize I am naked. Ripping the sheet up, I cover my chest while continuing to glare at him.

"I came to see if you were okay," he explains. "But this whole house smells of sex and cum, and I can't fucking think straight."

"And that is my problem, how?" I'm pissed at him for the omission I am just remembering, not matter how well he fucked me last night.

"I had the best sex of my life last night," he says angrily. "My knees were weak for over an hour after pounding the best pussy I have ever eaten or fucked. And you fell asleep with a vibrator in your pussy."

"Inside?"

"I let you sleep for an hour before I couldn't stand it. I had to take it out."

"So now you not only violate me while I am awake but asleep as well?"

Swinging my legs, I climb out of bed and move to the bathroom so I can finally brush my damn teeth. I leave the sheet behind, he's already seen me naked after all, and I don't have the mental capacity to care or argue with him right now. My entire life has been turned upside down in less than twenty-four fucking hours and I just need a moment of normal.

"Don't walk away from me, Addi," he growls behind me but I ignore him.

It only takes him a few seconds before he invades my space once more. I watch him from the corner of my eye. He is still the gorgeous man that swept me off my feet so easily, someone I wanted to get to know better, perhaps even build a life with. But now he is also the man that reminds me of a fucked-up deal I still don't understand. One thing I am certain of is that Mana isn't going to let either of us go.

"I need to know," he says softly.

"Know what?" I ask after spitting out my toothpaste and starting to adjust the water flow and heat in the shower.

Turning me around, he grabs me by the throat and walks me into the shower until my back hits the tiles. A woosh of air leaves me. His grip is firm but not harsh or constricting. His glare on the other hand is deathly.

"I want to know why the woman I fucked like a goddamned animal was asleep with a vibrator inside her pussy three hours later."

He is pissed off. Very. I wonder what he will do if I refuse to answer him. Where did that thought come from? All of this is so out of character for me it's not even a little bit funny. I would never let any man touch me or talk to me like this. Much less degrade me and share me like Kaleb and Mana did last night. What the fuck is wrong with me right now?

Not that my thoughts change my actions. Instead of answering Kaleb, I shake my head.

"Did I not fuck you hard enough?" he roars

punching the tile beside my head. I don't even flinch. Somehow I know Kaleb won't ever hurt me. Even when he's like this. Fury rages within him. "Was what Mana did and what I did not enough to sate and satisfy you? Do you need more? Tell me now."

His gaze is crazed as he scans my face for any kind of truth. After long moments he releases me, scrubbing his hand over his face.

"I can't let you go," he murmurs. "I've never been so obsessed about anything in my life but with you, it's like a fucking disease. Even if I have to share you with Mana, I will keep you."

A shudder works its way through me at the vehemence behind his words. He is both pained and determined and it's the mixture that has me telling him the truth.

"I had a dream," I say softly, still standing with my back against the wall. "You and Mana. Hands, cocks, lips. I woke up needy all over again even if I shouldn't."

"And now?" he asks, his voice low as he roves his ravenous gaze over me.

A whimper falls from lips unbidden as I rub my thighs together.

In the blink of an eye, Kaleb has me on my knees, his hands wrapped rashly in my hair. He pushes his soaking jeans down his hips to free his cock before prodding at my lips. Not for a single second do I ever contemplate pushing him away, fighting him, or saying no. I want this, I want him.

He spears me with his length, hitting the back of my throat and causing me to gag. I look up at him through my lashes, his face a mixture of pleasure and pain, starkness and beauty. His hips thrust forward, pushing his length down my throat over and over. My hand slips between my thighs, rubbing at my wet pussy.

Lost in the moment I don't realize Kaleb is watching me before he pulls me from the floor by my hair. A pained sound falls from my lips at the burn in my scalp but my protest falls on deaf ears. He drags me out of the bathroom, our bodies leaving a trail of water across the tiles and carpet before he pushes me down on my bed, face-first.

"I should leave you needy and dripping," Kaleb says above me as he keeps me pinned to the bed. "But I need to teach you a lesson." His palm connects with my wet ass cheek, stinging like a bitch. A sound I've never made before falls from my lips. "Such a pretty little whore," Kaleb whispers in my ear. "But you need to learn, pet, that we own all your orgasms now."

His cock spears me, hitting a perfect spot deep within, nearly ripping me apart. I don't remember feeling this last night but my body was already spent. He sets a brutal pace, fucking into me like a madman while he uses my hair to keep me trapped beneath him as leverage for his thrusts.

In the distance I hear vibrating before I feel something hard pressed against the rosette of my ass. Then it hits me, my fucking vibrator.

"No," I cry, squirming beneath him. "Kaleb, don't."

"But I will. And you'll take it like a good little whore and moan like you love it because you fucking will."

The vibrator slips into my ass as a tear tracks down my face. The sensations are too much to handle. Not once does Kaleb slow his pace or offer me a reprieve. My walls clamp down on his length as my vision blurs, the first orgasm stealing the air from my lungs.

"Again," he demands, moving my entire body up the bed.

"I can't," I mumble, hoping he will hear the defeat in my voice.

"Again, Adreana. And if you try to defy me, I will tie you to this bed and fuck you 'til you bleed."

His words tear at my insides, loosening something inside me I didn't know was there. One moment I am begging him to let me be, and the next I push my hips back into him, begging him for more.

"Fuck, you're perfect. No wonder Mana is as obsessed as I am."

Those words push me over the edge, my orgasm ripping through me as the vibration in my ass intensifies. His cock is ripped from within me and I almost cry at the loss.

"Christ, woman. You squirt like a fucking champion. It's like a waterfall." Kaleb curses and gloats at once. My legs and feet are wet, my face burning with embarrassment. "Mana is going to fucking love this."

He enters me once more, hips pumping furiously before he stills. I feel his cock kick inside my channel as he paints my walls with his seed. And I swear to every god there is, old and new, I didn't know I was capable of another orgasm but there it is, rippling through me and holding him in place.

Silence descends on us as we stay locked in position for what feels like an hour, both catching our breath, before Kaleb pulls both the vibrator and his cock from my body. Flipping me over, he smiles at me with dark eyes before pushing my knees to my chest. Using my hands, he positions me to hold myself in place before pushing my thighs apart. Neither of us speaks as he exposes me to his hungry gaze.

I am bare and vulnerable. I can feel the mixture of our cum slipping out of me and flowing between my ass cheeks.

"Stay."

I watch as he removes his cell from his pocket and snaps several pictures. Before making a call. I can vaguely hear Mana on the other end.

"She can't stay in Sinner's End, Mana. You started this. She needs to be at Harken. Permanently."

He listens to Mana's response I can't hear, nodding in agreement. "What the fuck is Sinner's End?

"We'll see you later."

Pocketing his phone, Kaleb returns to me, helping me off the bed before wrapping me in his muscular arms. I don't know what the fuck is going on right now but I know I need this. I love the rough, punishing sex. I crave the perceived violations and the dirty, filthy words. But I need this, too. His caress, his soft kisses on my face and against my hair. It soothes something inside I didn't know was there.

"Hello, sister."

The voice I know snaps us out of our intimate moment right before a loud booming sound rips through my home and my soul. Intense pain sears me. My stomach burns and it feels like my spinal cord is being ripped from my body.

Kaleb looks panicked and I can see his mouth working but I can't hear what he is saying. The world around me is blurry and I feel like I am floating on air. What the hell is happening?

Chapter Seventeen

Silver for the Boatman

Kaleb

I watch Addi order a coffee like she's a perfectly normal person. Her hands don't shake as she cradles her, "Tall, dark and handsome with three sugars, please," coffee in its environmentally friendly, recyclable cup. Her soft smile should light something inside me, but it doesn't.

Because after her deranged and damaged wraith of a sister turned up and blew her world to hell in two short words, *nothing* will feel normal to me ever again.

Addi dropped like a sack of potatoes, screaming her fucking head off all while she smiled at me, confused and tired. I didn't blame her in the least. The dichotomy of it all, broken and ruined, tortured and sweet, will never, ever leave my mind. "Fucking insanity" is the only term I can find to describe the way she smiled so serenely while bansheeing away like her soul was being ripped from within her.

That visual is burned into my soul, the last remnant of the woman I've come to love in such a short period, ruined by one of Mana's castaway toys.

All because of greed.

Possession.

I know enough about the man's fucked-up life to know the girls he plays with are changed. The more of him they take into their bodies—and I don't mean his cock—the less human they become. His drugs are the worst sort of addiction. A craving for forgetfulness.

Empty husks, soulless and hungry.

For nothingness.

Any priest will tell you that a blank mind invites the Devil. Mana's toys, once he discards them, appear to be fair game for any demonic possession wandering around out there. Because I can't imagine the man—demon, fucking whatever—that obsesses over possessing Addi with the same fucked-up fervor as me, that *man* wouldn't hurt her the way her sister has done. And Addi doesn't appear to remember a fucking thing about it at all.

I can't tell who to aim my rage at. Mana, for starting this shit by accident, or the sister whose envy, one of those lethal mothers of seven mortal sins, her greed—because who doesn't like to double on down with a little self-sabotage—fucked with her sister a hell of a lot.

Part of me hopes that little shit who smells like Emma but is nothing like her is dead inside. Because if she comes around and realizes what she's done, no amount of self-flagellation will solve that personal problem.

Mana's hand is in this, even if it's accidental. He's the cause of their blankness, their forgotten sins and fears and hurts that only mortals would ever fuck around with to find out.

Welcome to your own personal hell, bitches.

That's what the warning over the door to Harken should say. Because if they haven't found out before they cross that twisted, Gothic threshold, then they sure as fuck will by the time they leave.

Blank, empty minds. It's a curse, much so more than feeling everything the way I do. Like Mana. Even Bowen. Maybe the other hanger-on Mana collected. All minds free to claim. And when someone—fuck knows who—pushes into their heads and shoves down their souls, their little mortals seem to capitulate, happy to let someone lead while they fulfil their darkest, most fucked-up fantasies, and they aren't even in control.

It's the perfect blame system.

My demon did it.

It wasn't me, sir.

I didn't want to do it. They made me.

Like an episode of some fantastically fucked-up sitcom designed to satisfy violent cravings at the flick of a single button. And Mana has the motherfucking remote.

Now ... now, my precious, stunning, beautiful Addi is one of *them,* and she doesn't even know it. Mindless. One of the forgotten.

"Don't look so down. I got you one, too." Addi smiles up at me, her head tilted to one side like a Stepford fucking wife made to order.

Only, I want my OG Addi back.

"Adreana," I murmur, taking the coffee because it seems to make her happy. "Let's go back to the house. I think there's something you need to see."

Like several things. The scorch mark on the floor where she lay as her sister stood there and did nothing but gloat. An instant replay of the way the house's foundations and something below trembled with rage while she watched Addi writhe on the floor, screaming her soul out, smiling suffocatingly up at me like It. Was. All. Right.

None of this is fucking all right.

What scares me most is that I might not be the only one to claim this sister. So, I fucked her. As she showed me earlier in her bedroom, that apparently didn't mean as much as the weight I put on claiming her first. Maybe Mana holds that honor by proxy, fucked up as it is.

She's mine.

I sling an arm around her shoulders, drawing in a long breath as I press my lips to the top of her head, and scent something different. Something old. Something broken. And most certainly something not her.

"Home," I try again as she turns in my arms and angles her head for a kiss she doesn't return.

Like a goddamn robot.

"Harken," she whispers with a promise in her voice that isn't hers.

I sigh. "Harken it is."

Mana can fix this fuckup. Because I'm bringing the slops to his front door.

****

"The fuck did you do to her?" Mana roars in a whisper that rattles my bones nonetheless. His volume—or lack, thereof—is paired with the thick forearm braced across my throat.

Anyone lesser might fold before his fury.

I match him with that same dose of my own and raise his call with a perfect night I should have had with our girl. Yeah, ours. Because she belongs to both of us. Which means this is both our problem.

Bonus? We both get to fix this fuckup of mother-level proportions.

"Fuck you," I snarl, slapping him away like he's less than tinder-ready to flame.

Mana lets me go, and I hate him a little more for his version of leniency.

"She was horny as fuck when I got to her house. We fucked around. Had a bit of fun. The sister turned up. Said boo to the goose, literally two motherfucking words, and this shit happened. The earth rocked, the house shook. Then our girl turned into the ice princess."

"And the sister?" Mana watches me closely, not an inkling of shock or surprise written across his dark, archaic features that draws mortals to him like he's the god he'll never be.

"Gone. What else is there?" I snap, glaring at him.

"What else indeed." Mana lets out a soft laugh, the sort I hate most. His liquid smile and the way he licks his lips as he looks at me reminds me forcibly of the night at the bell tower.

"Do you ever have normal fucking sex?"

"Can you not swear for once?'

"What, a rich demon underlord cussing me out for my language?" I smirk. "Losing your grip on the overworld, old pal?"

His eyes narrow. "Where did you learn that term?"

"Turns out you don't keep the texts in your library as off limits as perhaps they should be," I coo, knowing it will incite the beast inside him. My soul calls for blood and since his is the shit that started this calamity, his is what I want.

Mana lets out a measured purr. "Don't try me, pup," he warns softly.

"Or what, you'll eat my dick?" I flip the bird for an extra visual, knowing this isn't helping with Addi, but I can't stop.

I don't want to fucking stop. If he isn't about to stake his claim, maybe my girl will be back. If he isn't there to stake his claim, then she's all mine.

Mana, however, puts on the brakes to our fight, overachiever that the fucker is. "What did you do?" he hisses between sharpened teeth, baring them to me.

I shrug. "I let my anger out."

"With *her*?"

"What? No. *No.* Man, you do you. It's not like we can't show our emotions with her. She's not going anywhere, Mana. Even before this, she was..."

"Perfect," we both whisper as Addi turns toward us, offering a benign smile that looks beyond fucking wrong spread across her face.

"What happened here?" Lethe strides past us, ignoring my growl and Mana's hiss. His white clothing is darker, more stained than usual. More like Bowen's, before he decided to advertise his death wish with a mantle of blood. "What did you do to her?" He whirls on us, panic written across his face. The ice-like facade of the pale man crumbles for the first time and he looks ... human, though we all know he's not. He crumples to his knees at her feet, rocking slightly and curling his hands around her calves, massaging them. "This is my fault," he moans, a broken ... well, a whatever. "My fault. I did this to you, my princess," he whispers, looking up at her as she ignores his suffering, like she's collecting all the pain in the room from each of us here.

My head snaps sideways as several things click at once.

"He's an angel," Mana murmurs. "And from what he said, it's likely he fucked her last night, or defiled her in some way. Who were you?" he calls to Lethe.

The tormented angel stares back at both of us while a blank, soulless Addi pets his hair.

"I don't know," he whispers brokenly. "I was supposed to protect her."

"Like a guardian angel." I frown at the cliche that's that bit too much.

"No. Nothing so mundane. I was to care for her, guide her. Love her as my own." His pale blue eyes, almost as clear but with more color than Bowen's, stare up at me with red rims. Tears track his dirty cheeks. "She was mine to protect. Just mine. And I ruined it."

I exchange a glance with Mana. He holds out a fist and I rock-paper-scissor him for it. Mana's rock loses to my paper.

He sighs. "Kid, you don't get to claim that. There's a whole lot more going on than you know. I've been keeping you at bay because I wasn't sure who you were but it looks like you might be joining us." He shrugs, like I did a moment before.

"Fun times," I mutter, shoving my hands in my pockets and watch the angel cry at her feet. A weeping angel...

There's something in that, but I can't put my finger on it.

"You don't understand," he whispers. "She was to be one of us. Like me."

"Lost?" I frown. I can't be the only one not getting this. Surely.

"Perfect," he whispers.

Mana snorts. "What the fuck ever. This isn't helping."

I nod my agreement. "Can your Chemist help?"

Mana watches me from the corner of his eye and raises one shoulder. "Maybe."

Shrugs for the win.

"No, you're not *listening*," Lethe shouts, shoving himself up so that even robot-Addi steps back. "She was *mine to protect*. Mine *to love*. But now I can't, and she can't. She was supposed to be one of us. Her soul was intact." His eyes are full of the sort of horror that understands everything. Like his penny dropped on a stupidly empty bank.

"And now it doesn't matter."

JADE MARSHALL AND RAVEN HUSH

Chapter Eighteen

A Little Bit Off

Adreana

Something is very wrong with me.

My mind keeps screaming over and over that something isn't right but it doesn't feel that way. I feel like me, just happier. It may be all the sex I've been having. You know, a decent orgasm can do wonders for anyone's disposition. And I have had quite a few in the last couple of days.

But I still feel ... off.

Things that would normally piss me off or irritate me are just brushed to the side today. It doesn't make a damn lick of sense but there it is.

I stare down at the large blonde man, the one who saved my life the other night, as tears pour from his eyes. He is kneeling on the thick rug of Mana's office floor, clinging to my leg, babbling about God only knows what. I know I should feel something, compassion or some shit like that, but I don't feel a damn thing. I honestly don't fucking care. How weird is that?

And then there is the other thing. This strange feeling that things are not quite what they seem. For example, I know the man kneeling at my feet is more than just a man. Curiosity surges through me as I take him in. He looks like any other man but he has an aura clinging to him that declares him to be more. I can actually see a light purple haze around him. Hell, Mana has one too, now that I'm looking, but his is a deep crimson color. What the hell is that about?

I turn my gaze toward Kaleb and even he has a blue haze around him. I think back, trying to remember if I did any drugs, but I know I didn't. At least not that I'm aware of. So, this can't be a drug-induced hallucination but I sure as shit can't explain what is happening right now. I shake my head, trying to clear all the random thoughts and finally focus on what is right in front of me.

"I want to get drunk," I announce loudly, drawing the attention of everyone present. I don't want to think too hard about what is wrong with me. It's a problem for another day. "I have been responsible for long enough. I want to get wasted and maybe even stoned."

"Addi," Kaleb starts, but Mana cuts him off.

"We open in an hour," Mana says. "But the bar is always open to you."

I smile brightly before turning on my heel. I slip between them, and march downstairs, leaving them to deal with whatever was just happening. I couldn't give a flying fuck right now. It's finally time for me to let loose.

Behind the bar is a pixie-sized woman with bright lime green hair, dressed in tight black jeans and a purple button-up shirt with enough of the buttons undone to show off her decent cleavage. She glares at me for a moment before speaking.

"Fuck off, Emma. You know we don't open for another hour."

"I'm not Emma. My name is Addi and I know what time you open. Mana said I could get a drink."

She looks me up and down before shaking her head. "You look like Emma. But not as … whorish."

"I like that people keep saying I'm not a whore," I sass with a chuckle. "My sister seems to have quite a reputation."

"That's the understatement of the year, girlie," she says, rolling her eyes. "What are you drinking?"

"Dealer's choice," I say, grabbing a seat. "All I know is I want to get shit-faced."

She chuckles before turning around to prepare whatever she is going to serve me. Rock music plays in the background but it's not loud enough to stop me from chatting with the bar lady. Now that I've kicked my sister out of my life and my house, I will need a new friend. Perhaps I can convince this pretty, snarky pixie to join me tonight.

"Are you working tonight?" I ask when she places a light blue drink in front of me.

"No," she replies with an eye roll. "I just like standing behind the bar and listening to assholes with corny pickup lines hit on me all night."

"All right." I chuckle, holding up my hands. "That was a stupid question."

"No shit." She wipes down the counter as I sip at the sweet and fruity but strong cocktail.

"Do you wanna get drunk with me?"

She gives me the side eye before replying. "I'm straight. And I need to work. I've got bills to pay."

Jumping off the chair, I stride to the middle of the dance floor before staring up at Mana's office window. I know he's watching me. I can feel his gaze even through the pane of glass and I can see his red haze through the tinted mirror finish.

"I'm taking…" I turn back to the woman. "What's your name?"

"Eve," she says with a frown.

"I'm taking Eve to get drunk with me!" I shout at the window. "But she still gets paid for her hours."

"Mana will never let that fly," she says with a shake of her head once I take my seat again.

The words have barely left her mouth before another man steps behind the bar. He was working the bar with Kaleb the last time I was here.

"Boss says you can go," he says to Eve.

She stares at me in shock while I clap my hands happily. That isn't like me, is it? This fucking happiness is getting to be a little much for me to handle.

"Get the lady a drink!" I say to the replacement barman, smiling like a crazy woman.

Eve walks around the bar until she is standing beside me. "How did you do that? Mana doesn't give anyone time off unless they are dead or dying."

"He likes me." I don't say anything else but I do slide her drink across the bar. "Do you really need to know why you have the night off, or are you going to smile while you drink for free and help me relax?"

"As long as I'm not paying, we can do whatever the fuck you want, girlie."

It doesn't take us long to finish the first round of drinks or the second and third as the volume on the music escalates and the sweaty, horny bodies of people start to fill the room. Everyone is dancing and laughing as I sling back tequila shots with my new friend Eve.

It's been a few hours of drinking, dancing, and even laughing with my soon-to-be bestie when hands land on my hips, pulling me against a muscular male chest. I should be worried about who is touching me but judging by the look on Eve's face, it can't be anyone except the man who rarely spends time in his own damn club. He is always sitting in his office behind his big desk, glaring at everyone that dares cross his threshold.

Taking a deep breath, I enjoy the scent I have come to associate with Mana, and Mana alone. Mint, mint, and freshly brewed coffee. I smile at Eve, who has stopped dancing to stare at us along with at least ten more people, before pressing my ass against his crotch with a wiggle. A broken moan falls from his lips before he speaks.

"Kaleb is acting like an old woman," he murmurs in my ear before placing a lingering kiss against my neck.

"Really?" I ask. Turning in his grasp I twine my arms around his neck and run my fingers through the thick hair that touches his collar. "And what is the old woman's problem?"

"He thinks there is something wrong with you."

I laugh loudly, my head thrown back. "There most certainly is," I reply honestly. "But I have decided to shelve that problem for tomorrow. Tonight, all I want to do is have some fun. Can we just do that?"

"You know?"

I huff. "Yes, Mana." I try to pull away but he has me firmly in his grasp. "I don't feel like myself. I'm too happy and shit that would usually bother me simply doesn't." I watch him as I speak, his frown deepening with every word. "But I have never felt this carefree and I am going to take advantage of that for tonight."

"Adreana…"

Taking the opportunity to catch him off guard, I lock my lips to his, kissing him with everything I have. A split-second passes before he kisses me back, devouring me. When he pulls away, I feel slightly lightheaded and weak-kneed but highly aroused. The smirk he wears is something I know used to irritate me but now I find charming.

Another mark against whatever the hell is happening to me right now.

"Come along then, ladies," Mana says, addressing me and then Eve. "Let's get fucked up."

Chapter Nineteen

A Pocketful of Ruin

Lethe

Mana's plan to seduce the girl who was designed for me is the worst fucking idea I've ever heard of. Any other night I might have been able to ignore his ploy. Play the wounded puppy part I've come to accept at his side, float through the haze my Maker left over for me and take the next sunrise in my stride.

Tonight, I want to rip his throat out and bathe in his blood before I tear everything in this sin-imbued place apart. I don't care if I terrify her, and something tells me as I step in front of the three of them—Mana, Adreana, and their spare—that my soulmate won't mind in the slightest.

She looks up at me with a faint amount of curiosity. "Are you joining us? No tears allowed after the way you cried all over me before," she admonishes sweetly.

I stare into her eyes, waxen like cerecloth, and shake my head. "You'll sleep in my bed tonight, my love."

She blinks at me long and slow, caught up in the dream state that creature put her in. Her hand detaches from Mana's as she takes a half-step forward. His growl is overridden by her half-smile that goes straight to my cock, but I ignore the pleasures of this mortal form.

Let her take her place as promised. I'll spend my immortality serving the pits of this hellish overworld if she's allowed to fulfil her fate.

I pray quietly, knowing her intended destiny without understanding my own, but giving it freely all the same. I don't receive an answer, nor do I expect one.

Adreana reaches me, her lips grazing the corner of my mouth, gliding along my cheek. "Come with us. *Lethe.*"

My name on her lips, stunted as though she pulled out the memory from a place long tucked away, leaves me aching.

"I will not share you." I cup her cheek, rubbing my thumb along her soft skin. Something flares in the depths of her eyes, an awareness maybe. I want more of a reaction from her at my touch, but this isn't the moan I know, the one my soul screams for, but the barest shade of one.

I promised I'd bring her back from whatever precipice she stands, whatever the cost.

"Not your choice, cupcake." Kaleb's meaty hand claps my back and I swear he leaves a mark.

Still cradling her gently, I throw an elbow back, hoping to connect with something important. Kaleb's yelp tells me I did, and I smile into her eyes.

Fake Adreana smiles back. "I'll sleep in your bed."

I wrap my hand around her nape, pulling her into my chest. "Good girl." I kiss her temple gently as she snuggles happily into my chest, apparently having forgotten Mana and her cohort altogether. The dark-haired man glowers at me. I give him my best reflective grin. "I'm happy to share the spoils. You get that one." I nod to the girl who manned the bar earlier.

She grins back weakly and spews a week's wages of tequila all over Mana's shoes.

He curses as I lift Adreana in my arms, and turn the first corridor I come to, anything to get away from

Mana's mess. Footsteps that don't belong to me echo mine. I turn my head to find Kaleb flanking me on one side, and Mana's pale pet on my other.

"I can manage her alone," I force out, gripping her tighter.

Adreana shuffles against my torso and bites my nipple.

Pain builds in my chest. I swallow it back like a treat, heedless of the tear that rolls down my cheek as she bites and licks and sucks. My cock goes on a rampage, straining against the white leather pants Mana dressed me in like his personal fuck toy for tonight's work. Not that I have any intention of working at Harken, not while Adreana remains in this state.

"You're such a little macho slut, aren't you?" Bowen coos, winding his fingers through her hair.

Kaleb slaps him away with the free hand not pinching his nose to stem the blood flowing there.

"Thanks." I give him a short nod.

"Not her, you." Bowen doesn't break his stride as he hops in front of us, walking backward. "She bites, you get hard. How much pain would it take for you to blow in your pants before you make it to your room? For you to fall to your knees while you hold her, *protect* her? Would you still be able to protect her then?"

Bowen's taunts grow while I count the steps between where I left Mana and my room, wondering if I'll get there before he unleashes hell and tries to snatch her back.

I don't know if I'm a match for the creature seething beneath his skin, or if he's a match for my beast, but tonight we might find out. I'm not sure if I'm disappointed or not when my door is in range and I push past Bowen with no further interference, laying Adreana out on my sheetless bed. I brush her hair back from her face tenderly, and push back onto my knees, settling in place.

"This is it?" I twist to find Kaleb staring down at me, his head tilted to one side. "The fuck did you do to earn Mana's punishment?"

His bewildered stare leaves me trying to see my spartan room through his eyes. The bed with no sheets, the single stool with my jacket draped over it. Stone floor, that, if I press my palms to their smooth, worn surfaces, weep with the tortured souls of those who screamed here for so many nights. They have been my nightly company through the long nights when this body refuses to sleep. Mana seems to share that problem when I've found him wandering the halls.

I shrug and turn back to Adreana. "I requested it."

"You—" Kaleb's mouth snaps shut, his teeth clanging together in an audible snick.

"—are a fucking maniac," Bowen finishes. "Mana will give you anything you ask for. Do you know that?"

I don't bother to turn back to the broken soul residing in the twisted thing that barely deigns to be called *human*. "It's not for me to ask."

"And yet you bring her here." Kaleb paces behind me. "At least at my place she'd be comfortable."

"Better than his rooms. Here, maybe we can bring her back."

His pacing stops. "How?"

I reach into my pocket and extract a small green vial. "This."

"No." A hand snatches it from my fist, and I don't need to look to know who took Mana's venom.

"That could work, you know," Bowen muses. "Clever pet."

He pats my head, massaging his fingers into my scalp. A deep pleasure radiates there, and for a few moments I forget the pain in my knees. A rumble works its way along my throat, almost escaping my mouth before I remember what we're supposed to be doing and shove him back.

"Glad you approve." I hold a hand out. "Kaleb?"

"ForgetMeKnot isn't the answer." He steps into my range of vision and folds his arms, staring down at her, his jaw set. "Addi, honey, you in there? Please?" he begs softly, dropping to his knees beside me. "Addi?" He reaches out to brush his knuckles across her cheeks, tracing over her lips.

A sadness emanates from him in this bleak place, and the stones sing all the louder. If he hears them, he says nothing at all, leaning over her, his head dipped like he might kiss her. I lean forward with him, ready to shove him back, but I don't need to as Bowen takes the moment of our dual distraction, snatching the vial of Mana's homemade drug and smashing it over Adreana's chest.

The green liquid covers her halter-neck top where it pools over her heart for a second. The fluid shimmers like a gemstone as I rear back, his throat in my hand.

"The fuck did you do—" I roar, but it's Kaleb's choked breath that gives me pause. I drop the interfering pale man, watching him carefully as he brushes himself off, and drop back to my knees to face Adreana's still form.

The emerald pool between her perfect breasts darkens, wavering. A darkness forms there, lifting from within, as though drawing poison from her. But as it extracts the shadow, Mana's drug sinks into her, right over her heart.

Adreana stiffens, the darkness taking a longer form over her. Bowen stiffens behind me, knives flashing in my periphery, then it's gone, along with her breath.

And then there's nothing at all.

I stare at her still form, the place where the drug sat no more than a tarnished stain between her breasts. Her chest doesn't rise, or fall, and her skin is the texture I associate with a doll's. Lifeless. I try to move, but I can't.

"Is she gone?" Kaleb croaks, like he's forcing the words out. He manages to place a hand on her skin and yanks it back. "She's freezing. Like—"

"Death."

The door to my room bursts inward. Mana stands there, barefoot, wearing only his black leather pants, his face twisted into an expression of pure horror.

"You fucking fools, you killed her."

Chapter Twenty

Loopholes and Lollipops

Mana

"I can't leave you alone for ten fucking minutes," I seethe, storming into Lethe's room, cell, whatever. "You should have been fucking. Or whipping, or sucking each other's cocks. Or even fighting. But you had to try to get the fucking soul out and you nearly took the wrong one." I shake my head, shoving Lethe back.

The destitute angel sprawls on his back, staring up at me. His lips part, but nothing comes out.

I snarl. "Fucking pathetic. And you," I round on Bowen. "You *know* better."

He shrugs. "I was curious."

"Cat. Killed. Curiosity. Those go together. When I wake her, we are having fun with all those things together," I warn him, letting my true promise enter my tone.

Kaleb, I ignore in his entirety.

Fucking mortals.

"You can bring her back?" Kaleb rises, gripping my shoulder.

I growl. "I was going to ignore you, my friend. Step away."

His survival instinct kicks in, and he drops his hand. *It'll do.*

I kneel on the hard mattress Lethe requested, straddling Addi, pleased when the bedding doesn't dip. My eyes closing, I listen to the weeping stones. Some of the oldest souls exist here and that helps me locate hers in the overpopulated map of Harken Asylum.

"Come back with me, Addi." I find her flitting from place to place, and frown. Usually souls cower in one spot, hiding, but she races on, leading me in a dance not so merry. "Where are you going, little toy?"

"Away," she whispers back, so close.

I open my eyes to find her sitting up, her lips mere millimetres from mine, her eyes wide open, and completely solid blue.

"Fuck," I snap, the shock ripping the curse from me.

Kaleb yelps and stumbles back, and Addi giggles. "Mortals, am I right?" She winds her body around mine, like a snake slithering out of her skin, only hers is still on—for now. Her limbs are liquid, and her coils are tight, restricting my air.

I swallow back the revulsion of what the thing I thought had left her could do with that sweet body and beautiful mind, how it could torture her, ruin her. I played with her, teased her, fucked about with her and her sister, and pretended not to care while I fell for the mortal girl who I'd give my immortal existence for … and now I don't know what's inside her or how to save her.

Addi winds her body around mine like a snake coiling about its dinner, her hands running across my chest in a frenzy. Her mouth fuses to my skin as she writhes and moans, making cooing, inhuman sounds that rip at my heart.

I want my little hell kitten back. But if I touch her, I'll kill her. Or worse.

"If any of you fuckers have an idea of what to do without hurting her, I'll take the advice," I grind out, stopping shy of begging. *Just.* "Fucking *help her.*"

Kaleb looks on helplessly, while Lethe tries to untangle Addi from the legs up, but she doesn't have control of her body and it doesn't work. Searing patches where her teeth fray my skin away in spots registers, but my pain was the least of my worries.

"Addi, honey, let Mana go. Let us help you," Kaleb starts, clasping her face and staring into her sightless eyes.

The solid blue that covers her entire eyes freaks him out as much as it does me.

"I don't want to stop," she says sweetly as she turns her face to his, her body tightening around mine. Something cracks, and the searing stops being skin deep and hits bone level.

"Fuck," I whisper, my body arching in an unnatural angle. "I left the underwo—"

Another crack, and I can't speak, can't breathe.

"Addi, let him go," Kaleb says urgently, joining Lethe in tugging at her body, pulling her this way and that as my vision grays, but neither can dislodge her inhuman strength from my body.

"Move," Bowen snaps. "Fuck me. Mana, you know better than to get in the way of a hungry succubus." He yanks out his phone and barks into it, snapping his fingers in front of her face three times, then again.

Addi stops.

Her coils loosen as he snaps his fingers again, getting right in her face. "Feeding time, my little friend. Ready?" He grabs her face, rubbing her nose right in his crotch.

Addi fucking coos right into him, her tongue whipping around him like he's a banana on ice cream day.

"Mmm, maybe if you're good we can play with that later, pretty fuck thing. But right now, get the fuck out of our girl and into the line down the hall. They're all yours. But you stay out of this room, and you follow the line all the way to the door. Once you're out, you're out. Don't come back. Here, or her home. Understand?"

Addi pouts. The blue haze leaves her eyes, and she slumps against me. Something giggling bounds about the roof of the room like an imp and out the door. Bowen whirls and locks it from the inside. Moans fill the corridor outside a second later followed by screams until the two are indistinguishable, a cacophony of terror and pleasure mingling.

Bowen smiles. "And that, ladies, is how you deal with a ravenous succubus."

I close my eyes and hug Addi to my chest as my bones pop back the way they're supposed to be. My breath comes easier. "Hells, Fallen. Did you empty my entire club?"

"Probably." He sounds uncaring. "You might need some extra staff, too, come morning. I wouldn't open the door until then." He claps his hands, a sly look on his face as he watches her rub against me with a tinge of residual horniness in her body from the possession. "What shall we do until then?"

Something cracks through the air that sounds like a palm hitting a cheek—face, not ass. Miraculously, it's not mine.

"Someone can spend that time telling me how the fuck that thing got in my house, and into me."

I laugh and hold Addi tighter, kissing her temples, the pleasure of knowing she's all right doubling when she doesn't fight me. "It's good to have you back, hell kitten."

"Ditto that." Kaleb joins us on the bed, snuggling beside me, and pulls her between us.

I don't argue, but no one else is getting on. "I don't know how that thing was in your house but I promise we'll find out." I open my eyes and find Addi staring between us. "What?"

"When did you two make up?" She frowns.

Kaleb licks his lips. "You don't remember a lot of what happened in the last hours, do you?" She shakes her head, and his face falls. "Fuck."

Mortals.

"Then that's exactly what we're going to do."

Kaleb turns his head to face me. "What? No," he protests.

It's the most pathetic protest I've ever heard.

I smile and reach out for a hand, uncaring whose I get. Bowen gives me his and I place it on Kaleb's cock, letting the ex-angel help him get it up.

"Nice and gentle now," I say softly, seductively, while Addi watches, her lips parting. "Our girl's been through a lot. Don't you think she needs contact, filling up? Tongues in her mouth and pussy? Doesn't she deserve some nice, hard cocks to fill her beautiful holes? And your sort of ... love, mortal?"

Her breath hitches as she swings to face Kaleb who blushes to the roots of his hair, a fantastic fucking distraction while my heart denies my own feelings that I don't want or need for her.

Liar, liar, immortal leather pants on fire.

I lean closer to Kaleb, bringing Addi's mouth to mine, kissing her close enough that his breath brushes my cheek while another man fondles his cock and balls.

He groans as I help Addi straddle us both, spreading her legs wide and giving us all access to her pussy, and pray I haven't just screwed up. An idea born of madness seeds deep in my mind, taking root and refusing to release me. This night could be hell ... or heaven, for all of us. Flipping her dress up, I run my hands over her panties, finding her wet and ready.

"Is this for us, Adreana?" I ask, a hint of sternness

entering my voice.

She drops her head, playing the part she knows I need her to play for him. *Such a fucking good girl.* I'm not sure if she can hear me, but my drug—my blood—is in her body, and even though everything in that gives me an element of control over her, I don't think the drug will react with her the way it does with everyone else. Tonight will be different. Besides, I want—I *need*—her to remember this. Us, together.

"Touch her." I capture Kaleb's hand, sliding it between her legs to rub her pussy.

She moans, and it's not just for show as we discover how to play her together. Addi's mouth finds his, but she surprises me when she pulls me in for a three-way kiss. Kaleb jerks back, but she's insistent. Our tongues tangle, moans filling the air. Another hand finds my cock and I don't know who it belongs to.

I ache with the lack of control over the situation, unsure who *is* in control or if we're all just riding the wave of intoxication that's Addi.

After all the teasing, the playing around, the stress of tonight, I'm ready to fuck her into oblivion.

"Suck me," I say to the disembodied hand working my cock, knowing I can't kill either of the angels. My magic bodily fluids don't work on my opposites that way. There's a second of hesitation that makes me wonder that it's not Bowen playing with me, and when a gentle touch frees me from my leather and laces and a long tongue strokes my length, I know Lethe finally joined us. I smile when Addi kisses me again. "And lick her," I murmur, positioning her in place right over me. The mouth hesitates again and I look over at Kaleb. "Do the honors?"

He grins, trailing a lazy hand down Addi's back to find her panties, bunching them tight and rips them clean from her body. Her gasp at his violence is worth it before Bowen and Lethe go to town on both of us, their mouths licking and sucking as I kiss the shit out of the girl who's consumed me for far too long. Passing her back and forth with Kaleb has me ready to blow.

"Don't stop," I warn the pair of angels licking my balls as I ready myself at her entrance and push inside her. Kaleb watches for a moment, fisting his length before I twist us to one side. I reach around, pulling him closer, and fit him to the same hole. "Together, hellspawn," I murmur. "Relax, hell kitten. Let us brand you as ours."

"Yours," she moans, tipping her head back and seeking Kaleb's mouth.

I swipe a drop of my pre-cum along her stomach, and when she doesn't writhe or scream, or blank, my innards scream my victory.

I know something about our girl that you don't know.

My head sings the little tune while Kaleb hums his approval, notching his cock next to mine and slamming hilt-deep alongside me.

We don't take it gentle with her, I'm not sure either of us can by then. We're drawn on by the frenzy of the night. Tongues lick all three of us as we work together, fucking her with one giant cock as she screams her pleasure to the weeping stones. The angels disgrace themselves, unsated and spent in their pants while they serve magnificently from below.

We paint the walls of Harken with our sin while a succubus rampages the halls and feasts in her honor, massacring everything in its path. Tomorrow will be a hell of a cleanup.

Tonight, I'm fucking a mortal I love with a man I hate and having my balls licked by two fallen angels.

Their penance will be pure pleasure and sufferance, and I'll enjoy their screams at my hands. As I come inside her, taking both Kaleb and Addi with me, I wonder if she will, too.

Chapter Twenty-One

Who I've Never Been

Adreana

For those of you that have never been possessed, let me explain a few things to you. First off, I have a massive gap in my memory. It's like missing part of a three-hour movie. Somehow the timeline is all screwed up. It's like I have been binge drinking for a week and now that I am sober, I have to fill in all the gaps, but I don't know where to start.

Second, I am ravenous. Not just for food but I swear to all that is holy—and probably unholy considering who I spend time with these days—that I have never been this fucking horny in my entire life. Mana and Kaleb have filled me with their cocks and their cum and I still want more.

"Rest now, little demon," Mana says with a crooked smile, a tinge of fondness in his voice. "There will be time for more fucking. But you need to regain your strength right now and we are trapped in here until the next sunrise."

I want to argue. I want to ask why we're trapped. I want to tell him he can't dictate what I feel or when I fuck but a sudden wave of fatigue swamps me and I can't even keep my eyes open.

Vivid, colorful dreams assault me. My parents, my sister, some long-lost friends. Happiness and joy fill me at seeing them all before sadness overwhelms me as each of them are ripped away from me in turn. I relive my parents' funeral for the millionth time. I see them in their coffins, I watch them be lowered into the ground, and I feel my heart shatter again and again before wrenching myself from the darkness that is my slumbering mind.

My body is overheating. Somehow all four of these massive men have fit themselves and me on the tiny mattress. I take in the room around me, rubbing at my chest. I don't know who lives down here but it's stark and depressing, enough to make me want to rage at the injustice of someone existing like this.

Behind me, Kaleb stirs before snoring softly once more. Tilting my head back slowly, I stare at Lethe, my makeshift pillow. Looking down, I find Bowen lying beneath my feet with a frown on his face. I wonder what fallen angels dream about. Do they even dream?

But it's Mana my gaze keeps returning to. I have never seen him so unguarded before. He looks like a normal, albeit hot, guy. His lips are parted and I fight the urge to kiss him. It's a strange and scary thing to realize, lying in a dank room in the bowels of Harken, but there it is.

All of us are as naked as the day we were born and usually I would try to cover up. But I feel a strange sense of comfort, a bone-deep connection, and I suddenly don't want to hide anything from any of them ever again. It's an epiphany I never thought I would have lying in bed with four men in the bowels of a building I have always hated visiting.

Everything in my mind is still in shambles from what happened to me, but I know three things for sure:
-- One, I need to find my sister. The little bitch fucking shot me or something and started this entire goddamned mess. I want to know what her damn problem is and find her the help she needs before she tries to finish what she started.

-- Two, I need to have an honest, open conversation with all the men sharing my body and this bed—if it can even be called that—before moving forward one more step.

-- Three, I am in love with Mana. Even though I swore I would never fall into his damn trap.

"I can hear your brain working," Mana says lowly, looking at me through barely opened eyes. "You should be sleeping."

I glare at him for cutting into my moment of inner reflection. I was having a moment, and he ruined it.

"I also need to eat," I whisper back, not wanting to wake the others. "And pee."

"I'll get you some food," Bowen says, before sliding from beneath my legs. "Mana is a horrid cook and I would prefer you not end up with food poisoning after everything you've just been through."

I watch his ass flex as he bends down to grab his pants where he discarded them earlier. I've had all four of them in some shape or form but I have only physically fucked Kaleb and Mana. I wonder if it would be different with Lethe or Bowen.

"Damn."

I turn my attention back to Mana, my brow raised in question.

He chuckles. "I never considered you'd be into this."

"This?"

"When I made that deal, I was mostly just fucking with you. And him," he says, nodding in Kaleb's direction with a grin. "But the way you just eye-fucked Bowen, I think you're more into being shared by the four of us than either of us ever could have imagined."

"Well, Mana," I say with a glare. "I have needs. I also happen to like sex and I won't be slut-shamed. Besides, you started this shit."

"He isn't trying to shame you," Lethe says, caressing my face and tucking my hair behind my ear. "He is in awe. You have been to hell and back these past few days, literally, and most women, most humans, would be crying in the corner, not contemplating what sex with a fallen deity would be like."

How the hell did he know what I was thinking? Can he read my mind? Can Mana?

"Your body tells us everything we need to know," Kaleb says behind me, his hand cupping my breast and tweaking my turgid nipple. "Your scent fills this tiny room every time you get aroused. Hell, I'm human—mostly—and I can smell it."

Well, that answers my question. Mana and Lethe watch raptly as Kaleb plays with my breast.

"Please stop," I say on a moan. "I'm trying to have a conversation."

"Talk all you want, babe. I'm not stopping you."

Mana chuckles darkly. "Why don't we compromise?"

"Compromise?" The word stutters across my lips, my arousal already climbing.

"Yes, dear," he replies with a dark gleam in his eyes. "Let us watch you fuck Lethe and then we can all talk together over breakfast."

"Why?" I may have already fallen for Mana, but I still don't trust him.

"Because I said so," he answers flatly. "Because I want to watch you take his cock. Lethe has wanted to fuck you since the moment he laid eyes on you. And because you know you want to."

There isn't a chance to deny his words as the three of them move quickly. Mana and Kaleb turn me flat on my back before they each grab a thigh, pulling my legs apart and exposing me to the angel who now stares down at me. He licks his lips as his gaze is locked on my exposed cunt. I watch in fascination as his semi-flaccid cock hardens and grows, pointing straight out at me.

"I know you like the taste of her pussy, Lethe, but now isn't the time for that," Mana laughs. "You can eat her out later. Or do you not want to feel her tight sheath gripping your cock when she orgasms?"

Lethe doesn't answer Mana, he doesn't even spare him a glance before bending down and bracing his weight over me, spearing me with his massive cock. It's nothing like Mana's horse dick but it is just as fulfilling, instantly hitting a spot deep inside me. Loud moans fall from my lips as he sets a punishing pace.

His hips swivel with every stroke into my heat, pushing me higher into pleasure. Mana and Kaleb release my legs as Lethe leans back on his haunches, staring at where his length disappears inside me.

My brain feels like soup and I can't concentrate on a single thing, my gaze bouncing between the three of them. Mana and Kaleb both have their thick cocks in hand, working the lengths in their fists as Lethe fucks me harder and faster. My breasts bounce on my chest, drawing their gaze and I can't help but cup the orbs in offering to them.

Lethe lifts my ass into the air, changing the angle of his thrusts, and I know this orgasm is going to wreck me.

"Come for Lethe, beautiful. Let him feel you milk his cock," Kaleb says, his hand a blur as he works his cock.

Mana's fingers find my clit, working mercilessly at the bundle of nerves, forcing me to comply to Kaleb's wishes. Lethe stills above me, his muscles taut as he joins me in ecstasy, both our bodies shivering with tremors as we orgasm together.

Kaleb's cum lands on my chest as Mana shoves Lethe out of the way, my fallen angel landing on his ass. A harsh slap lands on my pussy and my body convulses, my back arching off the bed. My scream rends the air. Mana repeats the action three more times before a second, more powerful orgasm seizes me. My legs shake as wetness seeps into the mattress below me.

"Did she just squirt?" Lethe asks in awe.

"Open your mouth, hell kitten," Mana says, not answering Lethe's question.

I comply immediately as Mana climbs over my chest and shoves his cock into my throat before coming with a roar.

Chapter Twenty-Two

The Sins of Us All

Lethe

Harken's walls drip with silence and death.

The wake of the succubus is worse than any of us could have imagined. Gore of every description sprays the stones that no longer speak. Their tears have been covered with the stench of ultimate, unhinged indulgence—and not just that of the creature we let roam the halls while we hid away and defiled the most beautiful sacrifice offered to us.

What I gave to her, before Mana shoved his way between us.

I could have sworn I saw something precious that stirred in the soul-deep pools of her eyes before he cut into our peace, something that wrapped itself around us. I love her, and for a moment, just a brief space in time, I thought perhaps she recognized the link between our souls long enough to love me back.

Now that connection has shattered, and all I was is … lesser. What I was meant to be for her *isn't* anymore. Yet here I kneel on the blood-drenched stones that refuse to chatter, drowned in their silence, scrubbing away at the souls of others that are too shell-shocked to recognize their own demise just yet.

Perhaps that is my penance in this place. To be the shepherd to these lost, pithy creatures and guide them into whatever afterlife they have earned for themselves when I can't remember the fate I created for myself.

"Wallowing gets you nowhere," Bowen coos

from his place above me where he scrubs lightly at the walls. His work does little but spray extra goop across the floor and at me, diluted by pink foamy suds.

Gray matter and glistening entrail remnants drip onto my filthy sleeves. I shake them off or try to, muttering to myself, but the color sticks. Soon enough I'll look like him, another tarnished, vagrant soul endlessly wandering this plane.

"What do you want?" I don't look up, unwilling to allow him to decorate my face with the same decrepit offering in a parody of Mana's playtime with our mutual obsession last night.

"Why do you let Mana treat you like you're worth less than a shit stain on his floor?" Bowen asks, dropping his darkly playful manner.

I blink at him. "Why do you suck his cock and let him treat you like his bitch?"

Bowen stares at me for a moment before his head tips back. He lets out a barking laugh that echoes along the corridor that should remain silent in this time of mourning. "Touche, little cherubin. It's good to know you have heart. You'll need it."

My eyes narrow. "What do you mean?"

His crooked smile comes too easy and sits far too wrong on his filthy face. "She's not safe with him. With either of them."

I scoff. "I suppose you think she is with you."

That smile sharpens, along with fangs that extend to dent his plush, bruised lips. "Oh no, broken one. She is most definitely not safe with me."

"What, then?" I swallow, unsure where he's leading with this line. That he called me "broken" hits too close to home, though I don't claim one of those, either. "What do you want?"

Bowen watches me for a long moment before he

drops to his knees at my side, his head bowed with grief, or at least the facade of it.

With him, I never know what to believe, and with his next words, I can't accept the risk, only the responsibility he places at my dirty, worthless feet.

"You must take her away. Because here, she'll die."

****

The eerie silence that follows my muted footsteps annoys me in ways I can't fathom as I stalk the lower halls. After hours of ruminating on Bowen's well-laid comment—no doubt as the man designed—and scrubbing every stone that refuses to give me its secrets, I follow my sense of unease to Harken's underbelly. Not in search of the woman who consumed me, but toward the demon I despise but cannot escape.

I find him strapped to the chair he hates almost as much as he hates himself, his mortal flesh already sagging as his life force drains away into glowing beakers lining the bench beside him. Tubes stick out at all angles from his body like something out of one of Kaleb's beloved horror movies.

The human might like to pretend he's normal, but his dark streak will be his undoing with Adreana. I know this as much as I know Bowen's disturbing words are true. But I cannot force myself to act on them.

Yet.

"How long?" I murmur, tracing one of the green, fluid-filled tubes with a fingertip as Mana deflates visibly before my eyes.

One finger flicks on the arm of the wooden chair that used to suck souls from this world via the conduits of electricity and a steel arm situated above his head, all in the name of therapy and lies. Now, it serves as a torture chamber for a demon who made a deal he cannot unmake.

The longer I stay on this plane, the greater clarity I gain, the more truths I understand.

My own penance for falling in love with the creature I am supposed to protect. *She will die here.* Now that I've heard those words, I will not easily forget them. But neither do I understand their meaning. Bowen, of course, chose not to illuminate me before he left Harken to do only deity knew what.

Adreana slept when I looked in on her, and I was loathe to wake her resting form. Her body draped over Kaleb's, and the human half-spawn winked at me as he toyed possessively with her hair. A growl embedded itself in my chest and I turned away before I ripped him apart, one hair at a time. By the time I stopped staring he passed out beside her, his humanity a weakness that left him vulnerable at such a time.

But shredding him would only earn me a tortured place beside Mana, and not with her.

My touch drifts from the tubes attached to the mechanical equipment draining the demon and over Mana's dulled flesh, the contact giving me the answers I seek with a finality that makes me want to rip my hand away. But he chooses to suffer alone, and that gives me a sort of pause that makes me want to stay and share his pain.

"It's as much an addiction for you as it is for them, isn't it?" I muse, brushing his thick, black hair back from his face.

A rumble of visions slides across my mind like a broken film: Adreana becoming a twisted puppet like her sister, unable to act for herself, dancing for him, with the crowd in his nightclub, each only an empty vessel.

Losing herself over and over, giving more of herself to him until there is nothing left of the woman I protect. Of the woman I love.

The demon gliding through her home at Sinner's End but unable to step foot across the hallowed ground beyond, bound by the tethers of the agreement with his master. A weakness amongst a plethora of strengths.

Mana stares up at me through listless eyes, and I wonder if he sees what I see. Regardless, I make my decision on the spot.

"She is so beautiful, but she's not for you. You understand that, don't you," I whisper as the Chemist does his rounds, making his passes across Mana's body, collecting his payment from the demon's body. He pays me no nevermind, as though he is not there at all. Even his body shifts, gliding semi-transparently across the floor. "He is not our concern," I wave him away as Mana's eyes seek out the only other assistance in the room that will not help him. "I'm taking what you want most, and you will not be able to reach her. You've shown yourself to me, you see." I touch his forehead in a sort of benediction, a blessing. "You can't cross by the graves beyond the house. And so that's where I will take her. Beyond your reach. And you will live this life and die without her." I press a kiss to his temple and whisper in his ear as his body flattens beneath mine, depleted.

"I won't let her die here because of you."

I walk out of his dungeon, the place where Mana has trapped himself with his little Chemist's toys, and stop to scoop Adreana from beneath Kaleb's arms. A light prayer carries an unnatural, deep sleep as I wish the human spawn sweet dreams, and carry her unscathed out of Harken to where Bowen has placed a car with a note tucked into the windscreen: *I'll see you soon.*

I smile at no one at all as the sun rises high above

Harken Asylum and shake my head, tucking Adreana into the back seat and wrapping a blanket around her prone, exhausted form. She curls into my touch, a sweet sigh eliciting from her tainted lips as I kiss her gently.

"No, Fallen. You won't."

Chapter Twenty-Three

Mirror, Mirror

Kaleb

Addi winds herself around me, her body sinuous and sweet as she glides against me, skin to skin, finally in my bed. I moan into her mouth, twirling my tongue with hers in a sensual dance. Her honeysuckle and vanilla taste twines with a spritz of lime from that first night in the club, a memory that lingers over us.

Warm, soft, all the things I love about her ... she's right there beneath me where she belongs. I pump my hips in time with hers, enjoying the simple pleasure of making love to the woman I adore.

"Aw. That's cute. Did you learn to do that in grade school?" Mana's caustic brand of sarcasm breaks into my peace.

"What?" I rouse out of the vision of her where I swear she's still beneath me, my cock encased in her liquid, warm heat, and spit out a mouthful of dank feathers from the old pillow on the mattress we used last night. "What the fuck...?" I freeze, looking down and find myself humping a puddle of Mana's leftover slop. "Jesus Christ." I swipe a hand over my cock, knowing this shit will never come off. Likely it'll stain my soul. "What the fuck is wrong with this place?"

Mana and Bowen burst into hysterics at my side, the shitty, deranged-as-fuck angel rolling around on the floor beside the bed. "Oh, human. That was funny. Do it again," he begs, sitting up like a puppy.

I lash a foot out at him that he catches instead of

dodging, and he licks one of my toes while I try to wriggle free, then sucks one. My cock, still covered in Mana's cold cum that reacts to the angel's fuckery and death grip, rises with a heady dose of unwanted arousal.

"Stop that. Fuck," I gasp.

My mouth hangs wide, recalling the last time the angel performed his dark magic on my body, though I've not had the destructive pleasure of his touch firsthand, until the last twenty-four hours. I yank at my leg while Mana watches, smirking and doing nothing, the fucktard, but Bowen refuses to release me, sucking and licking.

The image of him exactly where he is on his knees licking our balls while we fucked Addi senseless in a frenzy the night before is too much. I blow all over the angel's face, adding to his filth, and he licks my cum from his lips.

"Thank you." He bats his eyelashes at me.

I flop back onto the bed, shoving my pants back up and tucking my spent cock away. "The fuck is wrong with all of us?"

"So much," Mana muses. His face darkens. "It seems our rogue angel has done his little trick again."

I frown. "Done what?" I reach for Addi and find the bed empty. The vision of her was exactly that. "The fuck has he done?" I growl.

Bowen simpers at the floor. "Oh, God," he groans, running his hands over my ankles in a twisted form of worship. "Make that sound again."

I shake my head at the oversexed creature and kick him away. "Get off me. Where is she?" I direct that last at Mana.

He looks straight at me. "Sinner's End. Beyond my reach, hellspawn."

I snarl. "Looks like we have lots to talk about on the trip across town."

****

It turns out Mana has a door to Addi's damn house in his fucking study. Not his bedroom, because why would a demon need to sleep? And he fucks wherever he pleases, clearly.

He gestures me through with one hand, his eyes fathomless, almost sad. "I couldn't use it until she needed me," he whispers, and I swear the asshole chokes up.

Unable to give a shit, I walk across the floor of her room, the fragments of her childhood still evident in the traces of pink in her lace curtains, her handmade quilt, the crystal ornaments on her dresser. Her bed is still unmade from the last time she slept here, the scorch mark on the floor.

Mana follows me, his step cautious, but I have no time to waste on his precious moments.

"You said she's beyond your reach." I pause at her bedroom door, ready to stretch the hellspawn muscles he keeps telling me I have. "Where exactly does that end?"

His mouth thins into a tight, colorless line. "At the end of the graveyard. Not the entrance beside the house, the rusty little fence of the original land gifted to the first owners of Sinner's End."

I nod and take a step across the threshold to her room while he stays exactly where he is. It feels significant, somehow. "Why?"

"Why, what?" Bowen appears at his side stifling a yawn I'm almost certain is fake as fuck.

"Why was the land given to the first owners?" I gesture to the ancient house that creaks around us, adding its husky voice to the conversation.

Mana offers me a slight smile while Bowen stills.

"To ensure the covenant stays in place, of course."

I mimic the fallen angel's behavior. "What covenant?"

"To protect the juncture at Sinner's End where the Void meets." Mana sighs when I stare at him.

"English, please," I snap.

His lips lift in a silent snarl. "The covenant protects the owners of the house from the pull of the Void. In return they protect the Void from the prying talons of human and other kind who might wander in with intent, harmful, ignorant, or otherwise."

My chest tightens. "Are the sisters aware of this treaty?"

Mana shrugs. "Their parents were."

"And if it's broken?"

He smiles, a wicked thing that tightens my jeans with the sort of need I hate from the remnants of his sated pleasure I still wear by default, and a desperation to find Addi and take her the fuck out of here.

"If it's broken all bets are off, hellspawn. I'll claim every part of her and sacrifice her sister in her place as an offering to sate my master's hunger."

I stare at him, my mouth dry as my feet start to move.

"Run, run, spawny," Bowen taunts, his voice echoing through the house, following me into the graveyards beyond the rickety walls of Addi's accursed home. "Keep running. You won't find her."

Like hell I won't. But I promise you will never taste her when I do.

I leap between graves that date back hundreds of years, before the town proper was built, predating the asylum. My path careens wildly as I dart around an old crypt, its rusty gate swinging wide in a breeze that whips around me in an impotent dust devil, all rustling leaves that tear at my clothes. I bat the grasping tendrils away like they are hands, unsure what creatures Mana sent after me to stay my path, or what awaits Addi in the Void.

A lingering fear that the rift between reality and Mana's demonic plane reached the house and the asylum fizzles somewhere low in my gut, suffocating me from the inside out. I choke on stale air and the old souls long departed this life that linger in this frozen space with no home to return to as I stumble over the thin, rusted gate Mana mentioned and into the original hallowed lands of Sinner's End.

Beyond the limits the demon is able to tread. But me, with my human blood, can. Go figure the fuck out of that one. I don't make the rules, but I sure as hell intend to break every damn one in sight to find our girl.

"Addi," I call, my voice rough with need and fear. "*Addi.*"

I scan the area, the headstones here white and old, their names and dates worn away by time's cruel touch. No memory remains of the bones beneath our feet turned to dust.

I near a thick-trunked oak, trailing my fingers around its graffitied bark, the initials carved there. Had I been a few years younger, I might have declared my love for Addi thus, but that was a child's game. Though I don't deny it, my need, my craving for her, runs far deeper than a simple date, a quick fuck, and four initials and a heart embedded in the bark of a tree to withstand time's brutal kiss.

"She won't see you." Lethe leans against a cracked headstone, his ashy feet barely touching the moss-carpeted ground. "She's resting."

I plant myself and stare the not-angel down. "This isn't a game, Fallen. You don't know who you are or what you need to give to be able to play this game." *What the stakes are. Who you might lose.*

I understand Mana all too well. I know his games, how he plays. If only one of us walks away today, it must be Addi. That's what he wants. That's the offer. I thought I had a better deal with him than this but if it ensures her safety, I'll do it.

I don't, for a second, believe there is no loophole that prevents him from setting foot where I stand right now. A law, absolutely, but a loophole? No.

"Get her for me, please," I say in a low voice, keeping the threat clear and open.

Lethe frowns at me. "You're not like the others. You … love her."

"No shit," I snap. "Look, I'm running on short sleep. I don't know if you understand this, but he's playing you. Mana. Bowen. Whoever. They set you up for a joke. This isn't the best way to start your day, and you're fucking with mine. Give her back to me and we all go home. Play again tomorrow. Some other fucked-up game. Otherwise, we find out if you're as immortal as you think you are."

He smiles. "Or we find out if you will outlive the woman you love."

I stare at him.

Well, shit.

I swallow and nod. "There's that." He paces around in a broad circle and I match him, step for step, plotting the course. It can work, if I keep him distracted for twelve steps and if someone else is paying attention. If I'm not the decoy. "But do you love her as much as you think you do? How much of this isn't what you expected?"

Step, step, step.

He runs a hand through his hair, ruffling it the wrong way. "I don't know. I didn't expect anything."

Step, step.

I scoff. "Of course you did. How could you think you would get out of this without some form of recompense?" *Step. Step.* "What, just because Mana can't walk in, that you would walk out with the goods?"

"Don't talk about her that way!" *Step.* "She's not some product to be traded!"

Step.

I smile, genuine with him for the first time. "No, she's not." *Step.* I nod to the girl herself who appears behind him, shielding her eyes and confused as fuck, wearing the scent of each of us. *Claiming* each of us. That might be a dangerous thing, or it could save her life. *Step.* "Hey, Addi."

"Addi." Lethe forgets himself, whirling on the spot, and all bets are off. *Step.* "I didn't realize you were awake. Are you okay? I didn't know if you needed—"

"You piece of shit," Mana hisses in his ear as the angel crosses back into the borrowed territory where Sinner's End and the graveyard claims the demon can safely enter, pressing his black blade to Lethe's throat.

He forces the fallen angel to his knees in the dank earth that has seen the dust of a thousand souls or more these hundreds of years. I can feel their presence in the soil, as though they've never been released, or as though they're … close.

"The Void," I whisper, my lips cracked, dry.

Addi smiles at me, her eyes vacant once again.

"Hello, child of mine," she says as I stare into a face superimposed over the woman I love, that I only know from photographs but haven't ever met in person.

"Mother?" I croak.

JADE MARSHALL AND RAVEN HUSH

Chapter Twenty-Four

What I Take Back

Adreana

This time I know something is wrong. I'm myself, but I'm not. What in the ever-loving fuck is this bullshit, and why is this happening again? I try my best to shake off the twisty, dark feeling roiling inside me.

It takes me a moment to realize I am indeed outside. Naked. Although someone thankfully took the time to wrap me in a blanket. I stare up at the dark gray clouds obscuring the sun, and wonder idly what time it is. Not that it matters.

My body moves, but it's not me controlling my actions. Fear races through my system once more. Realization dawns on me as I finally comprehend what a marionette must feel like. Having my limbs moved without my permission. I'm here, but it's like I have been put on the back burner. Anger rages through me that I am yet again in this fucking situation.

"My boy," I hear myself say but it's not quite my voice. It is deeper, more gravelly.

"No!" Kaleb yells, his face pale as he stares at me. "You're dead. The dead don't come back."

"I'm here for you, Kaleb. You know Mommy loves you."

I feel dirty as the words leave my mouth. The thoughts swirling in my head are disturbing to say the least. No mother should think of her child that way, and I am revolted that this monster is using me to inflict more damage on her son.

"You're dead," he repeats, shaking his head.

"Yes, you killed me."

"No, no, no. It was an accident," Kaleb whispers.

He looks absolutely heartbroken.

"You know that's not true, baby. You hit that tree on purpose."

My mind is filled with images of the accident. The fight they were having, Kaleb telling her what they did behind closed doors was wrong. His mother touching him, trying to seduce him. The tree. The crash. Her body flung from the vehicle, shattering upon impact.

My heart aches for this younger version of Kaleb that his mother remembers. I want to hold him and tell him everything is okay. I want him to know nothing that happened is his fault.

"Shut up!" my own voice screams, my hands holding my head. "He isn't yours. You can't have him. He is mine."

"Addi?" Kaleb asks.

"Don't talk to her!" the thing currently controlling me hisses. "She isn't coming back."

The hell I'm not! I don't give a shit if I have to fight this bitch every day for the rest of my life, I won't just give in. I won't shut up and stay quiet while this hateful, horrid, spectre of a woman hurts one of the men I love.

Love?

One of the men?

What. The. Actual. Fuck.

Seems like being possessed or whatever I am is giving me clarity I didn't have before.

My body moves, stepping toward Kaleb. I can see him shake as my hand extends in his direction. I fight with everything I have to regain control, to not allow her to touch him. When the arm quickly lowers, I feel relief.

"You bitch!" she roars. "You can't keep me away from him."

"Let her go," Kaleb begs. "She didn't do anything."

"Another lie, Kaleb?" she asks. "She took your heart. You love her."

"I do. But that doesn't have anything to do with this."

"It does!" she says angrily. "You were supposed to love *me*. Only me. The bond between a mother and her son is special, and ours was more so than most."

"No," Kaleb chokes out. "You did things to me that no mother ever should. I didn't think I would ever be able to love someone the normal way. You broke something inside me before I even knew what that was."

"I loved you," she replies angrily.

"You abused me!" Kaleb cries out.

I feel the thing inside me doubt herself and I push. I push against the hold she has on me. I won't be held captive in my own damn body. The moment I feel her grasp on me start to slip I push even harder.

"Mana!" I scream, my voice my own once more.

I see his face just beyond the graveyard's gates, a dark blade pressed to Lethe's throat.

"Come to me, Addi," he calls out. "If you can make it here, you will be free of her."

I force myself to move, putting one foot in front of the other, but it is slow going. Kaleb's mother fights me for dominance, holding me back. My feet feel like they are filled with lead, making it hard to move them and win any ground.

"Let her go," Kaleb says, trying to pull me to Mana.

"Never!" the distorted voice erupts from me once more before I am able to fight back.

"You fucking bitch!" Mana roars. "If you weren't dead, I would kill you myself."

The entity shrinks back at his rage and I win a few steps before she tries to stop me again. I am two or three steps away from Mana and freedom from this bullshit.

"Lethe!" I cry out.

Mana glares at the angel on his knees. I know he can help me. Don't ask me how, I just do.

"Please."

Mana removes the blade from his neck and within the blink of an eye he stands before me. Gently, he swipes my hair out of my face.

"I'm sorry I did this to you," he whispers.

My heart cracks for the big man in front of me. There is so much I want to say to him, explain that I know in my heart he was only trying to keep me safe, but I can't. Inside my head, the entity shrieks long and hard at his touch. The tenuous grasp she had on me slips and I push past Lethe, jumping into Mana's arms.

I feel the last vestiges of her melt away the moment he catches me. Somehow, I know it has nothing to do with Mana but where he is standing. I breathe him in, enjoying the dark musky scent that always clings to him.

"I am so fucking done with all of this," I say a moment later, pushing out of Mana's grasp. "My sister tried to kill me, a succubus used me to get a free meal, and now I've had a dead woman in my head. I. Am. Fucking. Done."

With each word I poke Mana in the chest, driving my point home.

"I don't give a single flying fuck what wording you put into our deal, or whatever the fuck you did. I want out." I turn in a circle to glare at each of them in turn. "I am going home and I swear to everything that is holy if any of you show up in my house, in my room, I will fucking end you. I can't do this anymore."

"Addi," Lethe breathes out my name.

"Don't," I say holding up a hand. I pull the blanket tighter around my nudity. "I need time to figure out what the fuck is going on and having one or all of you around is not going to help. You all just keep distracting me with great sex."

Mana chuckles and I turn my glare on him. He holds his hand up in surrender. "You weren't complaining a couple of hours ago."

I shake my head sadly. "It's becoming more and more apparent that you aren't human, Mana," I say softly. "Or you would understand that sex is not enough. It's fun, but it's not something I consider when I'm making life-changing decisions."

He looks like I slapped him.

"Addi, you can't just walk away," he says lowly.

"You're hurting me," I say. A tear slips down my cheek. "All of you are. You're fighting each other constantly, and each time I end up as collateral. First my sister, then the succubus, and now this shit," I say waving my hand in the air. "How am I supposed to choose you, one or all, if you can't even get along for five fucking minutes? Each time one of you goes off on their own, I end up hurt."

"Adreana," Mana says, a stricken look on his face. "You know none of us ever meant to harm you."

"And yet we did," Kaleb cuts in.

I turn to face him, shocked that he agrees with me.

"Watch it, half-breed," Mana threatens.

"That's exactly what she's talking about, though. I say something you don't like, and you want to go twelve rounds. She says we all need to talk, and instead you try to fuck her into submission," Kaleb counters.

"You don't listen. You only have yourself in mind and fuck the consequences."

"We are all guilty," Lethe says, standing beside Kaleb. "I stole her to protect her but I never took into account what she wanted, what any of you wanted."

"Do you understand?" I ask Mana directly.

He shakes his head. "I can't let you go," he says softly.

"I'm going home, Mana. And you can't stop me."

"I love you," he says, his voice cracking. "We all love you."

His words pierce my heart. I love them all as well, but I can't keep doing this. They have turned my entire world upside down in a matter of days. And even though I've never felt so free, I have also never been so fucking terrified.

"If you love me," I say softly, "You'll let me go."

I watch as Mana falls to his knees in the mud, his head in his hands.

"Then go," he croaks.

I don't look back as I walk away, back into the house I grew up in. A place I no longer consider home, because none of my men are here. My shoulders shake as tears overwhelm me, my heart cracking wide open with every step away from Mana, Lethe, and Kaleb.

A loud wail pierces the air and I almost turn around to go back to them, to him. I feel Mana's pain all the way to my soul. I never thought he would say the words, but now that he has, I know nothing will ever be the same again.

I enter my yard through the back gate, wanting to go inside, shower, and cry myself to sleep more than I want my next breath. But I have never been that lucky. On my back porch sits Bowen with my beautiful Daisy, her head resting on his lap while he scratches behind her ear.

"I heard what you said," he says before I can speak. "I'm not here to try to talk you out of your decision. I just want to say something, and then I'll leave. Please."

I stare at him for long moments before nodding.

"I want you to know that we all love you, each in our own way. But of the four of us I am probably the one with the most damage." He looks up at the cloudy sky before returning his gaze to me. "When I fell, it broke something in me. I'm not like Lethe, who fell for a purpose. I fell because I was bored. I spent too much time on earth with the humans and one day I just couldn't go back."

"I don't know what you want me to say."

"I don't want you to say anything. Nothing you say can fix who or what I am."

"Then why are you telling me?" I ask with a frown.

"So, you know this is all my fault," he replies. "I mess with Mana and rile him up. I push Kaleb's buttons to see how he will react. I fuck with people."

"What did you do?" I whisper, a coldness wrapping around me that chills me to the bones.

"Emma came looking for you at Harken, the night in Mana's office."

"No!" I gasp.

"I led her upstairs before I joined you and Mana. I showed her what was happening, that Mana and Kaleb chose you over her."

"Why?"

"Because I was bored," he says, his voice flat. "I let the succubus into your house and told Lethe to take you through the graveyard. I didn't think you would leave."

"No," I cut in angrily. "You just thought it was fun to put my fucking life in danger!"

"You were never in danger," he replies.

"Oh, eat shit and die," I curse him out. "You can't say that, and you know it." I glare at him, breathing harshly.

"Punish me," he says, finally letting go of Daisy and climbing to his feet. "Cut me out, hate me, whatever it takes. But don't punish them. They love you."

"I can't believe a fucking word you say!" I cry out, slapping him across the face.

"Maybe not," he says softly. "But I'm not asking you to choose me. I'm telling you not to."

He turns and walks to the back gate before he stops.

"You're special, Adreana," he says, turning back to me. "Lethe fell for you. Mana has never made a deal to keep a woman for an eternity. And you healed Kaleb to the point where his heart can love again. Don't throw that away because of me."

He leaves through the gate but before he slips between the trees beyond, I call out to him.

"If I've done something for each of them, what did I do for you?"

A sad look crosses his face. "You made me feel the one emotion I've never felt before. Regret."

And then he is gone and I am alone with all this new information. What the fuck am I supposed to do now?

Chapter Twenty-Five

Blood on the Dotted Line

Mana

Mortals are fucking ridiculous.

I twirl the blackened blade forged of demon wrath between my fingers like it's a toy when its sheer presence burns my skin. This body is conditioned not to react to the sensation, no more than Lethe did when I pressed the hell-spawned metal to his throat.

Not that I would have hesitated to spill the Fallen's blood had it not been for the anguish in her eyes that shone through beyond the madness of her possession.

Kaleb took the proverbial cake with his display of twisted filial piety earlier that ruined everything we built together. Unfair, perhaps, but I'm not in a giving mood. Who would have thought the half-spawn had that much corruption in him? I'm surprised he can lift his mortal head, but perhaps he's a little closer to the caste he was birthed from than I expect. I won't underestimate him again.

My delusion comes hot on the heels of his knuckles flying at my face as Kaleb looses his rage on me, backing me into the crypt of some long-dusted human bones at the extremity of the graveyard beyond Adreana's house. I can feel the unsettled souls ekeing their way through the tainted soil. From the way Lethe twitches and Kaleb rages, I'm not alone in my assessment of this place.

Sinner's End is aptly named.

On any other day I might be interested in the

history of the house, but right now I'm more worried about keeping my face intact, having been on the receiving end of Kaleb's fury more than once in the last hour since Addi stalked away in her kittenesque rage.

"Are you scared she won't let you back into her house to play mommies and daddies?" I taunt him when his fists drop, relieved as my thigh aches from ducking blows that crash over my head and into the solid stone of the crypt wall beyond. "You did such a fabulous job the first time round," I drawl, just to dig the coffin nail deeper.

"We lost her because you can't tell a straight truth and keep your twisted dicks to yourself," Kaleb snarls back.

I raise an eyebrow, sucking in a slow breath to disguise how winded he's left me. *Insufferable mortal form.* "The little boy wants to play."

"I'll show you *little*—"

He stalks forward, and I prepare my thighs for another round of demon whack-a-mole.

"You'll never earn her back like this." Lethe's quiet voice saves me a beating as my thighs choose this moment to quiver and give out.

I sink against the stone wall at my back, trying to ignore the souls singing out to me for their eternal salvation—or damnation, whichever comes first—through its cracks, and raise a hand. "What do you mean, earn?"

Kaleb throws me a disgusted look. "Of course, you have no idea what it means to work for something," he spits at me.

A flash of red lances across his liquid-brown eyes before his fist lifts a second time. Something cracks in my ear. I duck belatedly, a second behind his action, to find his flesh planted in the stone beside my head.

"Bet that's worth it." I nod at his hand, relieved my noggin is still intact. Reinflating my head might be a touch more difficult than the rest of me under the Chemist's watch.

He grimaces. "Pity I have morals, or you'd be pureed demon." He shakes his hand out.

I stare at his unmarked flesh, then the deep rent in the stone. A coldness seeps through, tendrils of dead things reaching for me. A shiver wracks my frame as I push away from the wall and stumble forward under his watchful eye.

"Stop smirking. Once they taste your power, they'll be after you next," I mutter.

Kaleb examines his fist, testing the flex of his knuckles. "And if I put my hand through your head?"

I snort. "You'll be the first asshole I haunt. Earn?" I fix Lethe with a hard stare, motioning them out of the crypt.

Where the ancient site beyond Sinner's End drains me, it seems to give Kaleb power. An unsettling sensation leaks into my gut. There's a limit of sires in hell who attract the dead, and imbibe their souls like power. I doubt the fledgling hellspawn before me has any idea he's feeding from the crypt's cohort, but I have no intention of letting him absorb more of what he needs when I'm so weakened.

The angel watches us both with a brooding air more suited to the other Fallen whose significant absence does not escape me.

"Come on," he murmurs, offering his arm to me like a suitor of a bygone era.

I blink at him. "They say chivalry died a hideous death sometime around the sixties." Taking his arm, I limp out of the mausoleum.

"Is that how that quote goes?" Kaleb literally

yanks at his hair until it stands on end at my side. The power charge takes its toll on him, overextending his capacity.

"A different flavor from Harken, isn't it?" I mutter for his ears alone, answering his question with a question, knowing the angel beneath my shoulder misses nothing.

"What?" Kaleb snaps irritably.

I shake my head, torn between the amusement of seeing him high on demon lust for the first time, and worried for the toll it will exact on us all before the sun rises anew. "Should we adjourn to a safer haven?"

I offer my services and my home, as per fucking usual. I might as well open the asylum up to every stray who crosses my path, seeing as no one else seems to have one.

"We stay here," Lethe says simply as we breach fresh air.

I suck it in like life-giving brimstone while Kaleb deflates visibly at my side. Lethe says nothing, observing us with a fixed stare. Apparently, we both acquired a broader understanding of our unintended kin in the last hour. But my learning curve is far from over.

While Kaleb sags against a tombstone that refuses to speak to him, its residual soul long sucked dry by some preternatural creature, I find a patch of grass in the motherfucking sunshine.

"I'll be hugging a tree next." Lethe raises an eyebrow in a magnificent imitation of myself, and I concede a laugh. "Talk to me about Addi. What do we need to do to help her?"

His faint smile burgeons something warm within my chest cavity. "That's a fine start, demon," he murmurs, naming me for the first time.

The heat I crave extinguishes in an instant. I

wince. "Did you have to do that?"

"Always good to remind us of our origins."

"But not of our current state," I counter.

I'm unsure why I'm hosting a college level philosophy debate in a graveyard that's better suited to a frat house conversation that lacks the required copious amounts of alcohol for such a venture. Next, he'll be quoting *The Screwtape Letters* to me.

I shake my head. "Back on point," I encourage gently.

Kaleb glares at me and puts his fist through the dirt, rather than cracking headstones this time.

"I thought zombies came up from underneath." Lethe watches the interaction with interest, then clears his throat when I drum my fingers lightly on my knee. "Addi needs to see that she is the most important part of your lives. Mine also," he clarifies when Kaleb's glare intensifies.

"And we do this how?" he grouses, ripping up lawn in a perfectly round circle.

"We do what she asks, of course."

I study Lethe for a moment, running back through the accusations Addi leveled at us. What confounded me in the moment slams into me now a breath of clarity. If I were a praying man, I might offer gratitude. If I were a man.

That contemplation pushed aside, I focus on the task at hand—convincing our girl we need her for our survival. The longer I watch Lethe, the more obvious his faded glow becomes. Kaleb's anger roils pathetically beneath his flesh, and me … I'm a bomb of malicious intent waiting to explode. Our absent number, however, worries me the most. I wonder if Lethe has picked up on that little morsel, but decide to keep the thought to myself for the time being.

"We need to date her?" I ask delicately. "She said no sex." I keep my mouth in a straight line by pure determination alone.

"What I was trying to do when you busted in and fucked up my plans," Kaleb butts in.

"But there was sex involved," the Fallen drones, stealing the life out of the word.

"I had it handled."

"No, you didn't." Lethe fixes him with a stare. "Neither of you did. And I trespassed on her private territory, took from her when she wasn't even aware of my presence." He meets my eyes, his face flushed with guilt and a heady amount of arousal at the memory that surfaces all too fast.

My instinct to feed from him rises. I shove the unheeded desire back with a mammoth effort that deserves the sort of medal to win my girl back.

She's not a trophy.

But I fucking well deserve one.

"I'm impressed," I mutter under my breath at Lethe whose gaze shifts to mine.

The faintest hint of a smile tilts his lips before the emotion is wiped from his face. "Not the point," he berates me firmly.

My lips twitch, but I school my expression. "So, dates?"

He shakes his head. "No. It needs to be something more."

Kaleb glares between us, dark circles appearing beneath his eyes. I need to get him back to Harken before there's nothing left of him to return. "What, then, if not romance?"

I stare at the patterns he's torn into the earth beneath his hands. A mimicry of angel language and hellspeak, the two tongues mingled in a blasphemy that appeals to my mutilated sense of existence right now.

"How well can you grovel, Kaleb?" Lethe whispers coyly.

I swear my dick hardens on the spot. *So much for no sex.*

My gaze raises to meet his in challenge. "An obsession."

For the first time in over an hour, his hands still their destructive tendencies. Even Lethe perks up a bit from his odd version of eunni.

I mull over the term, tossing it around. It's not what she would choose for us, but then, Addi's preferences were tossed out the moment she rejected our love. No, this path suits us as a group.

Obsession will do.

JADE MARSHALL AND RAVEN HUSH

Chapter Twenty-Six

How the Fallen will Rise

Bowen

Stab, kick, stab, kick. Stab. One extra stab.

I have a nice rhythm going as I work my way through Harken, taking out the remaining staff and whores Mana likes to keep around. My little pep talk with Addi didn't really touch the surface. I did warn her but she wasn't listening to me, hell-bent on having someone to blame. I mean, I get it, she'd just found out I set her up to fail more times than not. A good backstabbing isn't just fun to pull off, it's immensely satisfying to see the end result. At least for the five seconds until the high wears off. Then it's back to the boredom of regular life. The guilt that eats me afterward.

Okay, not so much on that last part.

But Adreana draws me in, like all of them. I can't be her pet, as I already answer to one master. Having a mistress too seems counterintuitive. I'm not certain I can run between the two, so I must choose. My skewed sense of loyalty chooses the path of pain and self-flagellation.

Run from her I love, earn the hate from him I serve.

The path between Addi's house and the asylum is a simple walk, bereft of chance meetings. Thankfully, as I am in a murderous mood. That last part comes into play the moment I step within Harken's bounds. Adreana does that to me, brings out my worst.

I might have lied to her. It's not all boredom.

My last victim squeals and screams as I manage

to miss all his vital organs and hit only body cavity space. *What are the odds?* Even Mana wouldn't place a bet like that. I kneel beside him, placing my face level with the party boy who was just out for a good time and found himself … welp, in a spot of trouble, looking at the blood leaking from the extra orifices I've provided for him in the last moments.

I cup his face in my blood-slicked hands, caressing his cheeks with my thumbs, smearing freshly shed tears across his cheeks. "You're a regular here, aren't you?"

I vaguely remember his face from nights with Mana as his toy when he fed from the populace, peddling ForgetMeKnot on nights I wish I could forget.

"Yes," rasps the poor child who can't be more than five and twenty.

I nod sympathetically. "That's right. You're just in the wrong place at the wrong time, aren't you, my dear?" I smile gently, petting his cracked lips with my thumbs as he bleeds out onto the floor, his breaths withering. "Do you remember a certain girl? She came in here with her sister once. A pretty thing. Not the sister. She's a slut I'll deal with soon." My voice hardens. There's a task I'll treasure.

"You mean Emma?" He chokes in his haste to assist me, as I knew he would.

"Such a good boy. Yes, Emma is the slut. No, I want to talk about Adreana. Have you seen her?"

The poor child concentrates while his life force drips away a heartbeat at a time, soaking into the knees of my filthy gray pants. "Yes, I think so? She hangs out with the Man."

"With Mana," I correct as he coughs up half an organ's worth of blood. "Did you think she was pretty?"

He nods. "Of c-c-course," he splutters in his haste

to assist me.

"I understand," I whisper, though my heart hardens. No eyes deserve to watch her and see ever again. His haste will cost him. Plucking out his eyes is too good. A scarlet river wells over his lips and tumbles down his front, bubbling and gurgling. Looks like I hit a lung from the back. "Oh, dear. Shall I offer you an out? If you can crawl to that doorway before you die, I'll let you go. Would you like that?" He nods enthusiastically and I place a sweet kiss on his lips, licking up his blood and saliva. So much hope in that last breath. "Go on, off, you pop," I coo gently. "You can do it." I point him helpfully toward the door, maybe a dozen feet away, leaning down to whisper my tainted brand of encouragement in his ear. "You've got this, big boy."

What once would have been the perfect way to ensure a business professional hit their mark for the day or achieve that promotion, feel untouchable the day they need my power, becomes a tainted, twisted thing under the tutelage of my darkened essence.

My victim labors toward the door as I walk at his side, the owner with a dog off its leash, cheering him on in soft words and happy whispers as his blood leaks from his body.

"Oh my, you're so weak but it's just two more feet," I call when we're nearly there. His hands scrape piteously at the cement, so lightly he can't even scratch the flesh from his own palms. "But it's too much, isn't it? Too far. You did so well." I stroke his hair back from his face, placing his head on one side so he can see the doorway that's less than an arm's reach away, though he'll never achieve his escape. "So very close. It was never within your grasp but you tried so hard." His pale cheek rests in a small puddle of blood and drool, the rest already drained from his body, bloodshot eyes tilted up, staring, the last breath right there as I lean over him. "I'm here when you fail."

I seal my mouth over his and suck his soul from his body, swallowing him whole. Those eyes that watched her, saw her, lay blank and empty. Sightless.

He tastes like oranges and tequila. Unfulfilling. Unsatisfying as a replacement for my addiction to her.

There is no redemption for a broken being like me. Nothing that can stop my downward spiral. Why would I try? And so, I work my way through Harken, ending each life I discover and breathing in the souls, collecting them as payment for my master's return.

I'm sure he'll want them back before he ends me for all eternity.

A small mercy for a broken toy.

My vision blurs as I sway drunkenly and head into Harkin's underbelly for my next target. The souls fill me to the brim, overflowing my senses. Each pulses at the edges of my extremities, striving for freedom. This fleshy bond pulled out of the earth barely contains today's cache, but I won't let them go. I have a job to complete. One more life within Harken before Mana returns and receives the dues I must pay him.

I can't forget the Chemist.

And if my master loiters too long, I might return to Sinner's End and collect Addi.

Promises be damned.

Chapter Twenty-Seven

A Freedom So Fake

Adreana

Now that I have decided to get away from them, all of them, I need to examine my life. I need to reflect on everything that has happened and the part I played in it.

Grabbing a bottle of white wine and the biggest glass I can find, I make my way upstairs to my bedroom. I do my best to not look at the massive dark stain beside my bed as I walk into the bathroom. I open the warm water, adding in a copious amount of bubble bath, and lighting several candles, before lowering my body into the water. I fill the wineglass and drink half of it down before refilling again.

On the mat beside the bath, Daisy lies on the flat of her back, snoring loudly, making me smile.

I lay in the water, thinking back on everything that has happened. Trying to piece together where exactly things went wrong. If I can pinpoint the singular moment this entire fuckup started, I may be able to walk things back. Something. Anything.

I rub at the center of my chest, the pain radiating from my center. How the fuck did I end up here? In love with four men, one of whom I used to hate with every fiber of my being. I can still hear the pain in Mana's voice when he howled at my receding form earlier. It actually caused me physical pain to walk away from him, from them. But I must take care of myself before I end up dead because of something they did or didn't do.

And then there is Bowen. Motherfucking Bowen.

He could have just kept his mouth shut and left me in the dark. I honestly think I would have been better off.

Footsteps sound in my room before the bathroom door is pushed open.

"I told you I want to be alone."

I don't even turn to see who the hell it is. I don't want to see any of them. When there is no response, I turn my head and look over my shoulder. Shock courses through me right beside a massive dose of fear.

"Emma?"

She looks worse for wear. Her hair is piled on top of her head in a messy ponytail, she isn't wearing any makeup for the first time in probably five years, and she isn't dressed to the nines. Instead, she wears a powder pink tracksuit. She looks more like herself than she has in years, and it weirds me out.

"You're not welcome here either," I say once the shock wears off, turning away from her.

If she's here to try to kill me again, I would rather not look at her.

"I just want to talk," she says softly.

"There isn't a single thing you can say that I want to hear." My words are cold, callous, final. She may be my sister biologically but that is where our connection ends.

"Just let me say my peace, and I will be out of your life. Forever," she pleads softly.

My heart is already broken, torn to shreds from what I had to do earlier. And now I have to deal with her shit on top of everything? It's simpler to just let her talk, and then get rid of her, than arguing about whatever she wants for the next ten minutes.

"Fine. Make it quick."

I listen to her make her way into the bathroom, the low lighting keeping her partially hidden from me.

Daisy growls lowly and I can't help but smile. She has never been overly fond of Emma. I should have trusted her gut instead of believing in family loyalty.

Emma closes the toilet, taking a seat, her legs crossed. She stares at me for the longest time.

"You're different," she says softly.

"Your point?"

"You've always had my back. But something changed."

"I got tired of having to clean up your messes. I got tired of dragging your drugged-out ass out of Harken every few days. You needed some tough love," I explain even though I don't feel like she deserves my reasoning. "I couldn't have my own life because I was babysitting you and I just got tired of your shit."

I expect her to rage, to argue with everything I've said, but she nods her agreement.

"You just took over when Mom and Dad died. You took care of the house, took care of me. You did everything. Being responsible just came easier to you." I stare at her in shock and she gives me a sad smile. "You always did what was best for me so I didn't have to think," she whispers.

I continue to stare, my anger piquing deep inside my chest. "You had no fucking right to use me as a replacement parent," I seethe between clenched teeth.

"I know."

His words soothe my rage instantly. What the fuck is going on here?

"What is this?" I ask with a raised brow.

"I'm going to rehab," she says, watching me as she speaks. "It may be too little, too late for me to save our relationship but you deserve to know. I'm sorry. Not just for trying to kill you but for everything I've put you through the past few years."

"Emma, words are not going to fix what is wrong between us."

Once more, my palm goes to my chest and I rub hard against my breastbone. How is one person supposed to handle so much pain and heartache?

"I know," she says. "I need to do something big. I need to turn my life around and show you I can be there for you like you always have been for me."

"You tried to kill me."

"And of all the stupid things I've done, that's the one thing I really wish I could take back. But we both know life doesn't work that way."

"You expect me to simply believe you?"

"I expect my actions to prove my words. I expect this to be hard and it will take a long time before you want to be near me again," she replies earnestly. "But I need to do this before I end up in prison, or dead."

"I'm happy you want to get clean and do better for yourself, but I'm done with you," I say harshly, not wanting to listen to her anymore. "I've listened. You can leave now."

Emma stands, a tear tracking across her cheek. "I really am sorry, Addi. For everything."

She's almost out of the bathroom when I call out to her. "Emma?"

"Yes?"

"Don't ever fucking come back."

The door clicks closed softly and then I am alone again. Alone in the quickly cooling bathwater. Alone in my heartache that just seems to keep growing. Alone in life.

I have a choice on this last part, though. I can choose to stay away from Mana, Kaleb, Lethe, and even Bowen, or I can embrace what I might have with them. The thought of losing them makes my heart palpitate and my breathing accelerate. I don't want to lose them. Not a single one.

But then I remember the feeling of the darkness swimming in my soul, holding my mind and my body hostage. I still feel dirty after what happened in the graveyard, after the memories Kaleb's mother's ghost shared with me.

Having them, being with them, is never going to be simple.

As far as I know, the only human one is Kaleb. At least, that's from what I've seen so far.

I should really be running as fast as my legs will carry me. The only problem is, I want to run to Harken. To Mana. To Kaleb. To Lethe and Bowen.

But somehow, I feel like that will be the worst thing to do. Sitting upright, I pull my knees against my chest and allow my emotions to take over. The tears come fast and furious. I cry until I have the hiccups, the bubbles are gone, and the water is frigid.

Eventually, I force myself to move. After drying off I wrap myself in a bathrobe.

"Come on, Daisy," I say softly, padding down the hallway and into the lounge. "Tomorrow, we will find someone to replace the carpet. But, for tonight, we'll sleep on the pull-out couch."

It takes a minute to get the futon to work, but the moment it is open, Daisy jumps up, turns in circles for a bit before lying down, and resumes her snoring. I smile as I grab a pillow and blanket before going to sleep beside her. Maybe, if I'm lucky, the world will make more sense tomorrow.

JADE MARSHALL AND RAVEN HUSH

Chapter Twenty-Eight

A Knight of a Different Color

Kaleb

Walking sucks. My seething rage takes me as far as Harken's front gate. The moment I step inside the asylum's grounds, the debilitating energy leaves me devoid of just about everything. Already low in the energy department and held up by a previously untapped well of wrath I didn't know I possessed, I sag between Lethe and Mana who prop me up—no portaling allowed, as per Addi's orders.

We're on the straight and narrow, the three of us, a pact which lasts as long as that first step inside the building. No superpowers are required to sense the catastrophe that's occurred in our absence of Mana's domain. Blood and gore decorate every surface in an orgy of evidence even the weakest of detectives could find.

I stare at the dripping mess through slitted, blurry eyes. "I thought we cleaned this shit up." Even my voice comes out groggy.

"Some of us did," Lethe reprimands gently.

Some day I'ma gonna punch that fucker in the face hole for his holy-as-righteous-fuckerness.

Mana's jaw clicks in place. "Our fourth has gone on a little spree," he murmurs, trailing his fingertips through the glistening stream that drenches the walls of his home. I watch with a sort of morbid fascination as he brings those fingers to his lips and tastes them, a shudder wringing through him that seems to wick energy from his tall frame rather than give it as this place has always done for its master. "I'm not sure redemption is in his future."

Lethe shoots him a look, dropping one of my shoulders. "You did less for me, and here I stand beside you."

My knees hit the flagstone floor, soaking my leather pants in someone else's blood for the second time in two days. Pain reverberates along my thigh bones as they object to being dropped like twin sacks of shit.

"Ow." I roll my shoulders and try not to face-plant in the excess of goop as the angel and the demon host a silent, too-calm conversation over my head. "Someone wanna fill me in on what's happened here?"

Mana finally hoists me back to his level—*ha*—as still-cooling fluids pool around my ankles. "Bowen might have turned," he says delicately, striding through the carnage and dragging me with him as we head for the stairs.

"Turned … which way?" My brow crinkles as I stare upward to where his office waits on the third floor and pray that's not where we are headed. My legs aren't gonna make it. He tsks, and hits me with an unforgiving glare. "What?" I defend. "I'm fucking tired, all right?"

"Down." He shakes his head at me and places my hands on the slippery railing, tapping my shoulder with no little degree of condensation. "Catch up when you can."

He takes the stairs two at a time, though even I can see his legs shake through my double vision.

"Asshat," I mutter to them both as Lethe passes me, his tunnel-vision-focus single-minded as per freaking usual. At least he might keep Mana out of trouble by the time I make it to the basement.

Two and a half flights of stairs later, I know my assessment of the levels is wrong. Heading up might have been easier. I skid a few steps in the opposite direction, land on my ass, and try not to tumble headfirst onto the dirt floor imbibed with enough of Mana's spilled blood over his strange lifetime to host an army of demonic ghosts.

Spitting out some of my own saliva that mingles with the tang of metal, I sprawl beside the carcass of a familiar, albeit hated, form. The Chemist's face is caved in. His stretched, cruel features that always creeped me the fuck out are folded in on themselves like a flattened, origami figure. Even his body is sunken like whatever inhabited him has gotten ... out.

My shitty humor dissipates in a matter of seconds.

"The fuck happened here?" I mutter, crab-scuttling my freaked-out ass away from the horrific sight laid out like a preordained sacrifice at the base of the stairs.

"I'm not entirely sure." Mana crouches beside the Chemist's head. His hand hovers above the creature's— to call him a man is an insult to an entire species—face in a sort of benediction, though his forehead creases. "This work is something older than..."

"Me?" Bowen's thin, high-pitched voice turns both our heads.

Lethe steps up to flank us, a crossbow I don't recognize in his hands. I'd ask where he got the ancient weapon, but by the time my head turns to fix on Bowen's creepy ass, I no longer care.

The fallen angel—*how many freaking critters are there in this place?*—lounges sideways across Mana's torture chair like it's his personal playground. His bare feet are stained red to the ankles where they disappear into his equally filthy, once pristine gray leather trousers. The matching leather vest hangs in tatters, darker at the bottom like the inevitable sin he's indulged in for too long creeps from his waist up toward his heart where the original color of the tanned flesh still shows faintly through.

Pale skin flecked with dark splotches exposes an emaciated frame. Bones poke out at odd angles giving him a monstrous look. I have no idea what Bowen eats, but it's clearly been a long time since anything he's consumed has provided him with sustenance. His hand settles on the inside of his thigh, rubbing lightly just below his bulging crotch in an undeniably sexual manner.

Any sense of the purity he once held close no longer exists. If the being before us ever wore a halo, he'd find it a shit fit today.

"What are you doing?" Mana rises slowly, suppressing a wince though we all see it, as though the simple action pains him at bone-deep level.

I don't think our extended beat-on-each-other session is the reason for his anguish. Nor the death of the man who used to drain him for the dubious pleasure of his willing essence. His words register as I throw my legs in front of me and attempt to haul my rear off the floor, stumbling to a standing position. My first question might have been, "what have you done?" But that's not what Mana asked.

I spare him a sideways glance before returning my attention to the angel sprawled across his twisted throne. His fingers drift over his cock and he gives himself a hard tug, a sensual moan breaking free from his red-stained lips that lifts every hair on my body on end.

Bile rises along my throat to burn the back of my tongue. Addi's *no sex* rule suddenly seems that much more paramount. My fists clench but it's the dull flash between Mana's fingers of the damned black blade of his that stills me. *He means to end this.*

I'm not sure if Addi will forgive him for taking the angel's mortal life, or if he's beyond saving, but I can't let it happen this fast. Mana might, his wretched fucking soul doesn't need the clarity of my earthbound one. But I do.

"Why?" My voice thunders around the room, tinged with the desperation to save a life.

One single life as I realize just how silent Harken is.

The halls are quiet, except for the drips that echo alone each vacant corridor. The giant rooms, always filled with partygoers, last night's sluts, or staff, lay still.

Even the walls no longer speak. I had no idea I could hear them until I can't anymore.

Bowen did that. A single killing spree, and he's ended Mana's domain. My heart shatters fresh, and I know the answer to my unasked question as Lethe steps between us, forward and beyond.

A second flash, and the blade replaces the crossbow in his hand, a stark, reflectionless void against his fading but still present glow. An intimate, elegant weapon for a personal death.

The next look I cast Mana is filled with panic. *If he does this, he'll never be the same.*

But Mana's eyes are sad, and he shakes his head without returning my stare as my chest closes. A scream builds within my throat as Bowen answers me, stalling my warning by a hair's breadth. Too late.

And that's all it takes.

"Because I wanted to," he says simply.

Lethe raises the hellish blade and parts the taut skin at Bowen's throat, ending the fallen angel's existence.

My scream is as silent as the Void of Harken in that last moment before Mana's domain truly crumbles, and he loses the last cornerstone tethering his realm together.

Because the blood that pours from Bowen isn't red, like mine, or black like I might expect after the sin he's immersed himself in recently. It's a lurid green we all know so well. The color of ForgetMeKnot. Mana's blood, replacing his own.

Before the angel drains out on the floor, before Lethe turns to stare down at me in utter desolation I can't fix, the black blade clattering to the floor without an echo, Mana swears, pivoting on his heel without another word, and stalks away.

I'm left with a dead angel, one that wants to be that way, and an excess of a drug that could solve all my problems if only I'd bend the knee to crouch on the floor before Mana's broken throne and lap it up like the dog he trained me to be.

It's oh-so-fucking tempting.

Chapter Twenty-Nine

When They Call

Adreana

All around me is darkness. Fear creeps its way up my spine. I instinctively know I am not alone. Something caresses my neck, sending a full body shiver through me.

"It's too late," a voice whispers.

I feel the darkness wrap around me tighter, seeping into my bones and tainting my soul

"They are lost to you."

I know this disembodied voice is talking about my men. My lovers.

"No!" I shout into the void.

"Yes," the voice hisses in return. "You turned your back on them. Mana is done with you. And where he leads the rest will follow."

Panic envelops me, my throat closing in on itself, making it hard to breathe.

****

I wake with a scream. Daisy makes little noises of distress beside me and I gently rub her ears. It was just a nightmare. But if that's true, why do I still feel the darkness roiling inside me?

Swinging my legs off the edge of the pull-out couch, I start moving. My feet carry me quickly through the house I grew up in and I dress in haste. I can't stay here.

I may have been afraid of what was happening

between the five of us, but I am truly terrified of losing them. Come hell or high water, succubus, ghosts, mothers, demons, angels, or any number of godforsaken things, I now know where I belong.

I love them and they love me. And together we can conquer and survive anything.

Exiting through the front door, I take a deep breath of the fresh night air. And then I do the only thing I can think of.

I run.

Not away from what scares me. No. I run toward what I now know I can't live without.

I run to Mana.

I run to Kaleb.

I run to Lethe.

I run to Bowen.

I only hope I'm not too late.

Chapter Thirty

Silence in the Stones

Mana

I want to resurrect the angel and kill him all over again, but I left Hell for a reason, and not unaliving others is supposed to be a large part of my not-so-eternal reprieve.

Not that any of that is happening in this endless hell of my own making. I should never have left my sire's side in the first place. The hell was I thinking, pushing out on my own? Even a demon of my caliber isn't built to survive the sins of this plane. Apparently, imposter syndrome hits the most resilient of beasts in their weakest moments.

The ongoing torments of a population determined to tear themselves apart in their short lifespan is more than any demon can do in a thousand years, beating down on themselves in a perpetual cycle of hate and destruction and self-indulgent misery.

And love.

Of all this worthless mound of dirt has to offer, love is by far its most wretched construct. Because at the center of all the pain and longing to belong to one another is this lifelong fear of not only attaining someone's achievable desire but the fear daily—by the minute—of losing them. And now I have.

Adreana won't return to us. Me. Harken. The walls may as well crack and shatter now for the emptiness that fills each stone, and there are thousands. Hundreds of thousands. I should know. I used to be able to count the occupants imprisoned there.

But it seems my previous tenant ate their sins and consumed their wretched souls, leaving me the master of an empty kingdom.

Empty, worthless. Loveless.

All the things I hate about this world I now suffer alone. Without her.

"*Fuck*!" I roar, slamming my fists into my desk, through the hardwood.

Like the walls I imagined cracking a moment before, the surface splinters straight down the middle. The desk bows, tilting on its axis as the legs fail to hold the broken pieces together. Heedless of their capacity reached, I lean my full weight on my palms, hanging my head low. My shoulders scream with the strain, but I don't care.

Nothing matters anymore. Not the life I tried to build here, not the years put into this place, the meaningless existence within Harken that only took on some speck of value when *she* came into my life.

Now all that is extinguished and I'm too fucking tired to deal with the fallout. Hell, all I need is some mortal to join us and bring a squad of red and blue flashing lights to my door. Maybe they can cart me away to a safer place where I'll be given my own padded room, a jacket with no end, and a door no key can open from the inside.

My lips quirk. Hell on Earth. It sounds perfect.

Footsteps interrupt my reverie. I squeeze my eyes shut tight, blocking out the flat thuds like a toddler hiding behind his hands. But even that attempt at self-deception can't save me from myself as their owner draws ever closer.

Lethe has more sense than to approach me now. It must be Kaleb, ever senseless and suicidal.

"Leave me the fuck alone," I grouse, neck-deep in my bout of self-loathing, and enjoying my solitary bout of misery far too much.

Whoever said misery loves company was full of shit. Solitude is where it's at. Give me that white, round room and a two-way window where I can entertain a cohort of shrinks for the rest of my immortal existence.

"Mana. This place. You need to leave it." Addi's soft voice shreds through my defenses without an inch of effort. "Come with me."

I swing around to face her, untempered rage blazing from my every pore. "How the hell did you get in here?" I rasp, gripping the desk's shattered parts to keep myself from wrapping my hands around her neck and squeezing.

Or from kissing her and falling to my knees. If I do that, I'll never rise again.

She stares at me, the pulse at the base of her throat fluttering wildly. "I— the door was open. The floor. The walls..." She swallows, raising sanguine-coated fingertips to her face and turning them outward to show me. "What happened here?"

I smile at her, not an inch of humor left in me. "I grew too big for my own ego, little human," I say softly, watching that pulse beat out of time with my own. My hands itch to hold her tight, squeeze until that pulse slows, and tap out the rhythm to match mine until we both...

Stop.

Her breath catches as I find myself a mere breath from her lips, arched over her body, long steps from my desk where I left myself the last time I checked. Instead of cursing up a storm or retreating, I reach for her. When she doesn't back away, standing frozen like good prey always does, I fit my hand around her slim neck.

My thumb finds that spot I like, tapping gently as her body's beat increases. A deep snarl leaves me when she doesn't react the way I require.

Addi stares up at me, confusion, not fear, etching her stunning features. "What do you need?" she whispers, searching my face.

I should pull away, drop my hand, and let her go. I should tell her to leave this place and never return. Stay the hell away from the living dead who remain within the boundaries, because all we will do to her innocence is destroy her.

She cannot withstand our combined wrath unscathed. We will break her, like we ruined Bowen. He served me, and look at the outcome of that little venture.

A reaping, sin, and carnage.

The dirt floor of Harken bathed in my personal fluids, and not the fun sort.

I still have no idea how he managed to complete a full transfusion of his blood to mine, but right now isn't the time to contemplate his wicked ways.

And yet despite all Addi's declarations she'll stay away, here she is, within arm's reach. Within my hands.

"You said no sex, little hell kitten," I breathe, watching her eyes dilate as I close my hand around her delicate, mortal throat. "But you didn't say anything about death. What if I take us both back to my home, and show you what true pleasure is?"

A lie, because there's no way I'll take her to a place where she'll never escape. After today I'm not certain of the welcome I'll receive there when I do return. She could end up in the realm I left and I could be stuck … here.

Or nowhere.

The yawning pit of nothingness reserved for a greater sort of damnation than anything I've delivered with my eternal, unending soul.

"Do it," she breathes, crystaline eyes sparkling with tears of the horrors she's tread simply to get to me. "End us both and show me who you are, Mana. I want to know." Her head tips back as she offers me everything without a single thought otherwise.

The sound that grows within my chest isn't human.

"You have no idea what you're asking, little one." My thumb traces the line of her jaw. I could close my hand, collapse her windpipe, and crush her bone structure in one snap of my wrist. She'd feel pain for less than a second before she fell.

"Show me," she begs with all the purity of a freshly broken heart.

I swallow the need breeding within me. "Another time I would pull your chest open and drink from your bleeding heart while you still breathe," I serenade her, my voice low and seductive, the one I've used on a hundred-thousand souls ripe for devouring.

Addi quivers in my arms as her tears fall, but they aren't for herself. No, these tears—they're for the monster in me. She feels *sorry* for me.

The need to shred her flesh doubles, triples, until I'm fighting my own base nature to keep her alive in my hands. The simplest answer is to release her, turn around and throw myself from the window. I don't care if I wake on the ground, alive, in pain, or not at all.

As long as I don't take her with me.

I lean down and press a kiss to her pulse, gently, sweetly. "I will not bring that fate to you, Adreana." Before I can claim her mouth, I release her, though I don't back away, still inhaling the scent of her, needing to listen to the blood thrumming through her body. Needing to know she's real.

This day is beyond fucked up. If she's a hallucination, I won't be surprised. Right now, I'll take everything I can get.

"Because you love me." New tears coat her face, glazing her skin with anguish.

I smile gently. "You should go, sweet girl. This isn't the place for you. It never was."

Her lips tremble. "Are … are you throwing me out?"

The odd rearrangement of our first meeting, the meaning the same, the words twisted, sits strangely in my gut, though it sounds right.

"No, my love," I whisper to the girl I hated on sight and fell in love with for all the wrong reasons. "I'm not throwing you out. But this place is not safe for you. I am no longer your haven."

She sobs, great wracking moans that rattle her body, tearing her throat until she rasps before me. And still I smile at her, wishing I could feel her lips move under mine one more time.

"You are so beautiful, do you know that?" I trace a hand over her hair, not quite touching the silken locks. Undeserving to lay my hand on her again. "Find a human, Addi. Make love to a man who will adore you as you do him."

Horror fills her face. "You're rejecting me?" she whispers, her hands shaking as she reaches for me.

Sadness overwhelms me. "Love, I'm saying goodbye. This …you'll die with us."

"I don't care!" she fires back.

My smile returns. "I know, Love. You're so stunning when you're roused. Find yourself a good man. Find four, if that's what it takes."

"No one will replace you. Not ever." Her breath catches in her throat, her eyes reddening as her tears wash her skin clean with loss and salt.

"Perhaps."

I place my hands on her shoulders and lean in to press my lips to her temple. "Because I love you, I'll break your rules once more. Just once, my love."

Hope flares in her face, and my heart cracks. After this, there is no coming back. She'll hate me the way I once hated her.

"Goodbye, Adreana. My love."

My lips upon her skin are the last sacrilege, the final contact I need as I blink, shifting us to her room, lingering just long enough to see my loss reflected in her eyes, before I return to Harken and shatter the link with Sinner's End. Even I can't reestablish that connection now.

I stand in my study, leaning my back against the broken desk and face Kaleb who has finally dragged his horrified ass up to my level.

And he shouts the words at me that he wanted to scream downstairs, but couldn't then. Nothing, however, stops him from voicing those four tiny words right now.

"What did you do?" he demands, out of breath, out of everything.

Like me. All of us.

Lethe appears, wraithlike behind him. The angel places the black blade on the stone floor of my office. It makes no sound whatsoever.

I close my eyes, unable to face either of them for this next part. "I told her I loved her. And I took her home."

The finality of that simple phrase is enough to rock us all.

Kaleb slides to the floor, places his forehead on his knees, and cries. Lethe stares at the knife on the floor and looks torn between picking it up and joining his brother in arms.

Me? I stare out the window, and wonder how many souls I need to steal to make Harken sing again. One for every single stone in the foundations to the tip of the bell tower. Five hundred and fifty-four thousand, two hundred and twenty-three.

Enough to drown out my screams each night of why I let her go. Why I let myself be tortured and alone. Why I sent her into another's arms.

But first, I need to find myself a new Chemist. And figure out what the fuck Bowen did with the soul of my old one.

Chapter Thirty-One

The Bleakest Heart

Adreana

For long minutes I sit on the stained carpet of my bedroom floor, allowing myself to feel the true heart-wrenching pain flowing through me at Mana's rejection. And that's exactly what this shit is, no matter what he says.

He rejected me, pushed me away, and made decisions for more than just himself.

The longer I sit here, the worse it gets. Not the heartache, the anger. Rage claws its way up my throat until I am all but drowning in it. I know I made a decision out of fear but he is making his out of some twisted sense of chivalry or whatever the fuck he wants to call it. He is trying to protect me when he is really leaving me wide open. I no longer have anyone watching my back.

"Fuck!" I cry out, pulling at the strands of my hair.

What the hell am I going to do now? I know Mana can keep me out of Harken if he chooses. I grab my cell and dial Kaleb's number.

Disconnected.

Fuck me. Mana works fast.

I have no way to communicate with any of them if they choose not to talk to me. And I am getting angrier by the damn minute.

"Fuck hellspawn asshole!" I yell at the empty room, hurling my phone at the wall.

"Breaking your belongings will have no effect

whatsoever on Manashesh or his decisions."

The voice startles me and I scramble to my feet, fear thrumming through my veins. I stare at the man standing in the doorway. He looks exactly like Mana, all dark hair and pale skin, tall with broad shoulders, dressed in a perfectly tailored charcoal suit. The main difference is his yellow eyes, eyes that bore into my soul without asking for permission.

"Who the hell are you?" I ask, my voice softer than I intended.

He assesses me for long moments before speaking. "Perhaps this is a conversation better held in a less intimate setting. I haven't fucked a human in over twenty years and you are rather tempting. I can see why Manashesh is willing to lose everything for you."

A gasp leaves me at his words. Who the hell is this guy, and why does he think he can speak to me this way without any repercussions?

"I'll wait for you in the kitchen," he says before stalking away and leaving me dumbfounded.

I stare at the spot he vacated for long moments before making my way down the hall and into the kitchen. The moment I enter, I have a mini-stroke at the sight that greets me. My Daisy is wrestling on the floor with a dog twice her size. The thing that catches my attention is the fact that the other animal has parts of its skeleton exposed.

I want to call her to me, but the stranger cuts me off.

"Dogs need companionship, more than their master can offer," he says casually, never looking away from the dogs as they continue to play. "I never have less than two at a time or they get lonely."

"Are you lecturing me?" I ask.

The man laughs, a loud booming sound before

looking at me. "Not a lecture, my dear. Perhaps just some advice. With you spending all your days and nights at Harken, Daisy gets lonely."

I feel a pang of guilt in my chest. Daisy has been a lifeline to me for years and I have basically abandoned her. Taking a seat at the breakfast nook I stare at the stranger as he putters around my kitchen doing God knows what.

"To answer your earlier question, my name is Asmodeus. I am the sire of Manashesh, and a prince of Hell."

At his words, a fresh wave of fear crashes over me.

"You're Mana's father?" I ask, trying to tamp down on the terror I feel.

He smiles at me and I know I am not hiding a single fucking thing from him.

"You could say that," he replies, placing a cup of steaming, freshly brewed coffee in front of me. "You're going to need it for the conversation we will have."

I breathe in the aroma and allow it to soothe me for a moment.

"Why are you here?"

He chuckles. "Straight to the point. I like that about you." He takes a seat across from me and steeples his fingers. "I have been keeping an eye on Manashesh. Theirs is a bond between a sire and his spawned. I feel his emotions on some level. And for the longest time the only emotions I felt from him were boredom and disgust. But that changed recently."

"I don't understand."

"Of course you wouldn't," he replies with a derisive snort. "In the past few weeks, I have been bombarded by fear, anger, lust, confusion, and love. Do you know how that emotion makes my fucking skin crawl?"

His eyes glow yellow, his chest expanding to twice its size in front of my eyes. I know instinctively that I need to be careful of what I say and do if I want to survive this interaction.

"No," my reply is barely above a whisper.

"It's a vile thing that all humans chase to their own peril. Love," he sneers as he draws out the word like it's a curse. "And now my spawn has fallen into the same fucking trap. I granted him this time to see what he would become. I watched and prided myself on everything he did until you stumbled into his orbit."

I remain silent. First, because I'm not sure any words are required from me. Second, because I don't have a single fucking idea what I would say if called upon.

"Manashesh is willing to throw away the empire he has built. To return to our realm and his intended role, for you."

He glares at me, assessing, as if trying to find what makes me so special.

"And then…" He sighs, his eyes returning to their previous color and his size deflating, his anger leaves him just as fast as it arrived. "I felt you."

"What?" Disbelief coats my words.

He nods slowly. "When he left you here, sacrificing everything to make sure you would find your happiness, a bond snapped in place. A bond between yourself and I."

"That doesn't make sense."

"No shit. But there it is." He rubs a hand along his chin. "I felt your pain, anguish, your anger. But beneath all that was the pure love you hold not only for Manashesh but for the half-breed and the fallen angels as well."

"Half-breed?" I ask, confused.

"Mmmmh. Kaleb, I believe his mother named him. Another of my spawn."

"Shit," I mumble, trying to get my thoughts in order. "Does Mana know?"

"He suspects."

I stare at the demon, the prince of Hell sitting in my kitchen, lifting my cup and sipping from the coffee he made.

"Why are you telling me this?' I ask the only question I really want the answer to.

He tilts his head to the side, studying me like an insect under a microscope. My skin pebbles beneath his gaze and it takes every ounce of self-control not to squirm.

"I want you to return to Manashesh."

"Mana doesn't want me anymore. He rejected me, not the other way around."

"He doesn't have the final say. You do. I do."

I let his words sink in, my heart aching at the thought.

"I don't know if I want to be with him if he doesn't feel the same."

"Fucking humans," Asmodeus curses loudly. "Did you not hear a single word I said? He loves you. He feels so deeply for you he will return to Hell to give you the chance at a life he wants you to have without him."

Fuck. Hearing those words for the second time settles something inside me.

"And what do I have to give up?"

"Everything," he replies with a dark grin. "You will bind your body, heart, and soul to Manashesh for eternity. You will rule Harken and the surrounding area by his side, corrupting souls and sending them to me when the time is right."

"What about Kaleb and—"

He cuts me off with a wave of his hand. "Those are my spawn's decisions. But know, if you choose to do this, there will be no going back. You can't run away when things get difficult. You will be bound to him forever."

"Forever?"

"The ceremony to bind you will also bind your life force. You will never die, never age, never be able to leave him."

One would think this decision should be hard. That I would take hours to work through each of our interactions and everything that has happened. But it's not. It's the easiest decision I have ever made.

"Yes."

"Yes?" he asks with a raised brow.

"I agree. But…"

"There will be no caveats," he cuts in.

"I want to keep him," I say pointing at the hellhound now sleeping beside Daisy. "You were right. She needs a companion."

His laughter booms through my home once more. "I can see why he likes you."

Asmodeus snaps his fingers. The change is instant. One moment I am sitting in my kitchen, dressed in yoga pants and sneakers, the next I am standing on the main dance floor in Harken, dressed in a blood-red gown that caresses my skin and clings to every curve.

"Manashesh!" Asmodeus's voice carries through every inch of Harken.

I'm not sure Mana heard him. Silence reigns, enveloping us. It's soul-deep, and I have never heard the building sound so … dead. There has always been movement, sound. Now, there is nothing.

A moment later, Mana appears from a hallway,

flanked by Lethe and Kaleb. His gaze collides with mine, anger flaring.

"Sire," he says lowly, stopping a few steps away.

Kaleb and Lethe keep their eyes downcast as they stop behind him.

"Spawn."

I remain at Asmodeus's side, waiting to see how this will play out. But beneath the lush material of the dress, my legs shake with the effort of standing still and not running to them.

"How can I serve?" Mana asks stiffly.

Asmodeus chuckles. "So demure. Your woman has more backbone than the three of you combined."

I watch Mana bristle at his father's words and a low sound builds in the back of my throat. The demon beside me laughs loudly, drawing the gazes of all three men. Shock scrolls across their features.

"This is what I mean," he explains. "She has been terrified since the moment she met me, yet she bargains and disapproves."

"Leave her alone," Mana says lowly.

"Why? She is here by her own choice."

"Does she know the cost of her choice?" Lethe asks.

"I do," I say before Asmodeus can reply with some non-answer. "I'm here to claim what is mine."

"There is nothing here for you," Mana says flatly, not looking at me.

"She will be bound to you," Asmodeus cuts in before I can reply. "Or she will die in front of you."

Chapter Thirty-Two

I Am My Father's Son

Mana

Fuck my father, and fuck this place. My soul burns with the need to tear the building apart, reduce every stone to ash, and my sire to bare bones his dog can chew on for the next millennia while I hang my head and beg her forgiveness.

Not that she'd accept my groveling, from the look on her face as she stares me down. Her head is held high and she looks nothing less than a queen of this realm in a dress I know my father designed not for her but for my mother when he offered her the same deal. The deal she politely declined, and walked away.

He didn't speak for the next forty years until her bones were interred beneath the earth, but his reign during that time had never been crueler. I wonder if I will be as pathetic or harsher than my sire should I perpetuate that same cycle.

The other part that raises every hackle in me is the way my sire looks at the woman I'll bend the knee for over an eternity. Like if I don't take up the mantle, he'll willingly replace the mother who walked away from us both with her. And from the way she watches me, then him, my little hell queen is all too willing.

"How much of a fight did you put up?" I snarl, stalking forward into her space.

My unblessed father watches on, the benevolent god of the realm bestowing motherfucking favors upon his chosen favorites.

Her chin raises, defiance pouring from her in waves that hits me at chest height. "None."

My snarl transforms into a growl as I reach her, winding her hair around my fist, and jerk her into me. "An eternity of reaping souls for my father. Those were the terms, were they not?" I give her a little shake. "Are you ready to become the worst murderess in history, kitten? For him?" My body arches over hers.

Where once she might have slapped me, or bowed back, cried, or pulled away, now she stands serene at my show-ponying.

She shakes her head once, the smallest, prettiest smile curving her lips. "For you."

Breath leaves me as I fall to my knees, my hands closing around her shoulders as I take her to the floor, still stained with the recently reaped souls. Addi's legs tangle with mine, her thighs parting until she straddles me. I hold her over my hips, keeping our mouths level.

"There's no going back," I whisper, searching her eyes that will be mortal for only moments more if this is what she intends to follow through with. His plan. "Do you understand that? We will be bound, the three of us, forever."

"Six," she corrects me, that smile wreaking havoc on my system.

I frown. "Don't follow."

Addi holds up a delicate hand, listing us off. "You, me, him," she rolls her eyes and folds down three fingers while I lean in and suck on the tip of the next. She bats at my nose. "Stop that. Kaleb, Lethe, and—" She looks over my shoulder and frowns. "Where's Bowen?"

"Shit." I bare my teeth. *Way to ruin the moment.* Daddy Dearest might have a cog he didn't plan on here. "He's, uh…" I stall, unsure how to break it to her, and not rip her heart out in the process. "You know the carnage you waded through on the way to my office?" I wince, knowing how callous my words sound.

Her brow creases. I hate the motion, but I'm holding her weight and can't shift to glide my hands over her skin like I want.

She nods. "Yes…"

"He—"

"I killed him," Lethe cuts in, kneeling beside us and offers her that goddamn black blade I never took from him.

Fucking hell, I should have taken it back from him earlier instead of wallowing and planning for a future that no longer matters. Perhaps it never did. If she doesn't end us all right now, he likely will in a bout of self-delusional loathing, like his brother from another angel mother. A cringeworthy oxymoron at best, but I don't have time to dwell on it.

"Why?" Addi's head tilts to one side as she observes Lethe quietly.

He watches her in return and offers up the knife, saying nothing else. Their conversation happens at a nonverbal level that kills me inside, because I don't have that depth of connection with her. *Yet*.

But my fear goes unfounded. She won't hurt him, not physically at least.

Calloused fingers lift the blade from Lethe's outstretched hand. Addi stares up at Kaleb, reading his face. Not a word passes between them, either.

The entire beginning of our impromptu ceremony goes down in utter silence while my father fucking well *glows* over my girl like he's proud of her for stepping up, rather than admitting he forced her hand.

Kaleb lifts Lethe's fingers and presses a gentle kiss to the angel's palm that leaves my blood firing. A simple, small slice that leaves his palm welling in a pool of garnet, and then he gestures for mine. Hard, dark eyes lance through me as he captures my wrist. The tip of the blade, demon-forged steel digs into my flesh.

For a moment, I wonder if he intends to stab straight through my palm, but instead he only pierces the skin, then leans in and kisses my mouth, flicking his tongue across my lips. A roar fills my existence though he hasn't spoken yet. Green-tinged blood fills my palm as Lethe's does his.

I clutch Addi to me tightly, one-handed, though she's so damn slight one hand is more than enough. The trials of the last weeks have taken their toll on my little mortal. Her legs dangle over my hips, the heat of her warming my groin. Every shift slices a driving awareness through me. Sire present or not, the moment the ceremony is complete, she's ours.

When our lips part, I breathe in Kaleb's scent, recognizing him as my own. I nod, meeting his eyes, but the challenge that's always been there merges into something else. A binding by our Maker, sharing our lover together. His hand releases mine, and the blade presses to his own palm.

Shaking my head, my lips part, but I'm unwilling to break the strange silence that tethers us. Lethe reaches out, nuzzling Kaleb's thigh with plush lips. He's already as high as we are on need, driven by the desire emanating from the female encircled between us all. He makes the cut on Kaleb's palm, flicking his tongue out to lick a slice of exposed torso skin when the spawn's shirt rides up.

There's barely enough air to make my next inhale for the desire emanating from the angel coiled around our feet. His free hand wraps around my calf and Addi's ankle where he rubs his fingers over her bare skin beneath the dress that has seconds of life left at the most, marking her with his scent, or maybe the reverse is true.

Kaleb's contribution is complete as we all hold our hands together, drawn by the inexplicable force that is Adreana. The other two might not know this ritual, but it's written on their bones, along with her name, and mine. We claimed them before they were birthed, and we will own them long after this world withers and burns.

Together we make a clover of our palms, a cup we tilt, red and green swirling together in a mix of forgetfulness and life and obsession.

A pledge made by necessity, and offered by force.

A cup she drinks from of her own free will, draining though my cock strains, fit to rupture as my blood mingles with the others in a scarlet and serpentine trail over her breasts, ruining the dress.

The roar in my ears stills. Somewhere above us, Harken's bell tolls. Once. Loud enough for the world to hear.

Beneath it all, my father laughs and leans back to watch the show, his mortal facade merging with the monster beneath. We all have one of those, but there will be time to explore that with her later. For now, Adreana is ours.

The thickness in my chest expands past the point of feasibility. Our hands part as I grip her dress and shred it with my claws, uncaring if I slice through her skin to her bones. Uncaring of the scream that leaves her lips, the way her thighs pulse around my cocks.

I no longer have to be careful of the woman I've obsessed over for too many nights. She's mine now, and I'll destroy her at will with two other immortals. Shatter her, ruin her, and put her back together the way I want. Because this is my fucked-up version of love. Obsession. Need.

Now, she'll take us all.

Chapter Thirty-Three

As Above, So Below

Lethe

I sink lower on the floor the moment the bell tolls above us, filling Harken with its message. The monster's father laughs, and the deal is signed in the blood she imbibes, unaware Mana claimed hers in the process, slicing her thigh open on the inside.

I thought I wanted to lick her before but now my saliva drips down my chin. I stare at the full, crimson beads tinged with the slightest hint of green that swirls within, like bloodstone. She's filled with a mix of us all. A keening fills the room, and I realize after a moment it comes from me.

Rough hands catch my hair, yanking my head back. Kaleb stares down into my face, his eyes hard, unforgiving. The angles of his face flicker as he becomes what he's truly supposed to be in the presence of his sire.

"Will you serve her?" he rasps, his throat working as his flesh darkens, hardens.

My hands tremble around their legs as I nod, unable to make more than the base sounds with my own mouth that refuses to work under duress. My balls ache as I rub myself against Mana's leg, humping him like a dog in heat.

I expect him to fling me off in my desperation, but instead he winds some of the ribbons he made of her dress around my nape, and together they push my face between her legs.

Her tainted blood smears my lips, my cheeks,

flows into my mouth as they rub my face into her pussy, blessedly bare. I mumble my thanks, pray at the altar of my goddess as I lick and suck and drink the benediction she offers.

The moans above me are cut off as Mana snarls something, but I stop listening at that point. Kaleb is my God, guiding my mouth over her, his touch as unforgiving as his darkening eyes. Not allowing me a single breath, he uses my mouth to rub her to orgasm while I fight for air into my lungs, giving her everything.

Mana's bulge strains next to my face, Kaleb's cock insistent behind my head. I'm trapped in my position of servitude as he works me hard, calloused fingers digging into the back of my head as her legs soften, and liquid heat floods my mouth.

Ambrosia coats my tongue as she comes, her sounds muffled above but I don't need to hear them to know we've done our job. I flounder behind me, stretching back for Kaleb. His hand clasps mine in a death grip, cracking my knuckles in recognition and reward as he lets me have coveted air.

Only for a second as his mouth crashes over mine, his tongue brutally invading my mouth. "Well done, little fallen," he hisses, his newly forked tongue stroking my lips as pre-cum leaks from my cock. "Do you want your reward now?" His eyes glow with fervor, fingers fisted tight in my hair.

I nod as his other hand strays to the front of his pants, and I watch with eager eyes, my mouth falling open, already covered with her slick. It only seems fair that I share him, too.

"Wait." Mana's command cracks over us, stilling everything.

"Please," I beg, turning my eyes on him. I trail the hand still wrapped around his leg and hers up his thigh.

"Master," I plead, lost, and needing his direction.

His eyes soften as he gazes down at me. "This is what you want?" The question there gives me hope.

I nod, arching back as he pets my head, giving me his thumb to suck. "Errvoolll," I say logically around his digit.

Mana laughs softly. "As you wish," he whispers, his eyes alight like Kaleb's. He leans down and kisses me gently. "Would you like to fuck her after we've had our turn? Once we've brutalized her, you can sully her with your filthy angel seed?"

The offer has me fit to burst. "Last, please," I gasp, tears prickling my eyes. "May I lick you?"

He shakes his head, amusement filling his face as he takes his thumb away, leaving me empty. "No. But you may warm him until she's ready." He turns away and dismisses me.

I blink, bereft, until Kaleb's touch finds my jaw, firm but not cruel.

"Open," he commands, his thick cock in his hand. "Don't make me come, and don't touch yourself. Just hold me to the root. I don't care if you can't breathe." His gentle stroke along my cheek with his cockhead belies the violence of his words.

Air leaves my lungs at the prospect. I walk forward on my knees, but he backs off a step, laughing at me following him across the floor. The humiliation of his actions leaves me a panting mess. He turns and backs up.

Behind him, Mana has Addi laid out over his arm, scraping his claws across her body, shredding her skin one cut at a time as she screams and writhes in pain and pleasure, begging him to stop and pleading for him to keep going at once.

The image burns into my mind, and I can't tear myself away, not even for Kaleb's delicious cock right before my face.

"You like watching them?" he muses, catching my jaw again and tapping his cock over my lips.

Angling us so we can both watch, he feeds his cock into my mouth until the head taps the back of my throat. His pubes rub my lips, then his hard, flat stomach, and his balls love-kiss my chin, nestling there.

I moan around the mouthful, swallowing as gently as I can on the intrusion, getting used to the feel of a cock in my mouth, the salty, earthy taste of him. My tongue traces gently along his length until he groans, cupping the back of my head with both hands and holding me in place.

Barely able to breathe, my eyes strain as I watch Mana destroy our girl, bleeding her sweetly over his arm, licking her blood. As her body heals, he does it again, whispering tender sins into her lips. When he's tired of that he brings out his cocks, fitting one to her cunt and one to her asshole, doing her dry. Then he pushes inside to the music of her screams, pain, and pleasure at once in a way that makes Kaleb's cock swell in my mouth. His balls tighten and he grips my scalp with ferocious pressure.

Certain I'll swallow his load as he curses and jerks his hips in my mouth, I soften my tongue and let my mouth fill with saliva, coating him. Plenty dribbles out the corners of my mouth and along my chin. He shudders, but miraculously he holds his wad.

Settling, he cradles my head to his balls, letting me soak him lovingly as we watch them fuck. Mana takes his time, seducing her with his brand of sin. Addi's voice long goes hoarse before she comes again and again for him before he screams her name, lighting Harken with his roar.

The stones awaken, the very earth rattles beneath

the asylum's foundations. Somewhere, a bell that isn't of this place tolls and again his father laughs, disappearing as his son completes his mating ritual and claims his queen for an eternity.

Kaleb moans softly as her pussy is vacated. He taps my cheeks with his fingertips and smiles as I release him. "Thank you," he murmurs, leaning down to spit into my mouth.

I swallow the taste of him with a moan, my hands drifting to my thighs.

"None of that." Mana kicks my hands away from my cock as I whine.

Ribbons of her red dress lace my arms behind my back in an intricate tie, and by the time he's done, Mana's hard again. He walks back around to my front and holds both cocks in his hands, pumping them before my mouth. "Open."

I stare at the two cocks, one hard and ridged in every way, the other flatter and leaf like, cupping his other length like a sleeve. "Too big," I whisper, slightly horrified at the thought of him forcing both into my mouth, remembering how he shredded her and wonder if he'll do the same to me.

If I'll survive the wrath of his mating.

His eyes glow black and fathomless. "Open," he repeats in warning, taking his rigid cock and pressing them to my mouth.

Eyes wide and panic flowing through me like air, I part my lips. He slides inside my mouth, coated with Addi's blood and both their cum mingling around his strange surfaces. I work each with my tongue, exploring, tracing as he groans in pure pleasure. When I bob my head, he slaps my face with his other cock hard enough to sting.

"None of that," he snaps. "Warm me. Clean me.

When I want to coat you in my seed, I will."

I nod gently, unwilling to earn another humiliation from him. Knees aching, I set about my task as Kaleb fucks Addi into the floor. Their moans fill the newly awakened stones, giving them life. I moan with them, my pants saturated. I'm not sure if I've already ejaculated, but there's enough fluid leaking from me to make a single strand to the floor.

"Filthy little angel," Mana murmurs, toying with my hair. His gentle caresses earn him hums from my throat until he moans and pulls me closer into an embrace where his other cock closes its odd shape to cup my throat. "Fuck, you're my new favorite toy. Every night we're playing like this until I tire of you. Kaleb can make a playground of your ass and Addi will suck you until you're screaming silently. Understand your place, cherubin?"

I nod, spreading my legs wider.

His cocks pulse as Kaleb roars. Addi's scream hits me along with a dual stream of cum as Mana pulls out of my mouth and coats my face, throat, and chest with enough demon seed to water an elephant. His mark drips from me in ownership as he stands over me. A pleased smile curves his arched lips.

"Now," he whispers. "You may defile her."

I whimper my thanks in Tongues, unable to think as I crawl my dripping form away from him, my arms still laced behind me, and climb awkwardly aboard her ruined body. Scars and slashes cover her perfect flesh, each healing within seconds. Her eyes stare dozily up at me, but she's half gone after Mana fed her pussy his cum.

I'll make sure she remembers this part, though.

Where the others were rough, I whisper. Where they tore her and plundered, I lick, coating her with more of Mana's cum as his seed transfers from my body to hers. The sticky layer binds us as I bring her to orgasm after orgasm, both of us writhing. Finally, Kaleb pulls down my pants and reaches around to grip my cock, leaving my hands bound at my back.

It's all I can do after the endless hours of teasing not to scream at the slightest touch when I can't get myself off.

"Make a playground out of your ass, I believe he said?" the hellspawn whispers in my ear.

He scoops his palm through the puddle of Mana's copious cum from the hollow of Addi's stomach and reaches behind me, lathering my hole with his fingers. My cock strains impossibly.

"I'll blow in seconds," I gasp.

"Then you'll be fucking her for as long as it takes her to come again," he hisses cruelly.

I moan as he fingers my asshole and I find her hole with my cock, sliding into her sopping cunt. Addi's walls close around me, sucking me into her tight warmth. I groan at the feeling that grows as Kaleb's fingers disappear only to be replaced with his cock.

He licks my neck languidly, lovingly. "I'd say I'll go easy on you, angel, but—" He slams balls-deep in one endless ream that thrusts me to the hilt into her. "It's a filthy fucking lie."

Kaleb rails me, setting the tempo we fuck at. I have no control at all, cradling Addi to me as she flops in my arms. Her screams meld to my lips as I try to kiss her gently but my cock swells impossibly, stretching her with my thickness from the inside out.

I needn't have worried as within seconds she's coming again. One orgasm tumbles into another. My ass contracts as my balls draw up, and I milk the fuck out of the cock invading me by pure instinct as I pour everything I have into the woman I love.

Together, we fall. Together, we breathe.

I close my eyes and let them catch me as I tremble, impaled between them. Seed leaks down my legs and along my ass crack, leaving me feeling used and filthy and loved. My hammering heart promises any more of this shit and it'll give out, but a cold, impassive voice brings me back too abruptly.

"Isn't this … sweet."

I stare at the high polish on the black patent shoes and wonder idly how Mana kept the damn things so clean with so many fluids floating around. Then the high pitch registers, and I look up into a face that drops all the pleasure from the world.

Dressed in black leather that floats about him like a mist, his skin tainted with shades that roil beneath his flesh, hair grayed out and eyes a solid obsidian of expired sin, stands the fallen I ended with a blackened blade. A single pale scar marrs his shadowed form where I sliced his throat open.

Death came for him and he returned the favor, wearing his clothes and taking his form. His attention shifts to Adreana, and he reaches out a hand.

The reaper has come for her, and his name is Bowen.

Chapter Thirty-Four

One Without

Adreana

Have you ever lived a moment and it felt like everything was in high speed? That's what the last hour of my life feels like. I can't pinpoint a single moment that stands out above the rest because everything is one big blur, like my life has become a flowing river with no distinguishable characters.

What I do know is that the sex has gone from intense and passionate to indescribable. Mana finally has free reign to fuck me the way he has always intended, and I swear I thought I was going to die from the pleasure overload.

All three of my men have taken their time fucking me, binding us together. And even though I love them all, there is an ache in my heart that won't fade. A longing for the person not here anymore. My soul calls out to Bowen. I don't know what happened exactly, but I do know that Lethe wouldn't have killed them if there had been any other choice.

It's like my heart conjures him out of nothing. One minute I am panting, trying to get back to being myself, Lethe still resting between my spread thighs. The next, Bowen stands above us.

The joy I feel in this moment is tantamount to another orgasm. My soul sings at the sight of him even if he looks different. I take in the changes. His eyes are the color of onyx, a pale slash scarring his throat. His hair and wings have darkened to near pitch-black and his clothing reflects the change.

It's strange in a sense to see my angel, who is always so snarky and sarcastic, standing there stoically. A seriousness I never would have thought possible for Bowen radiates from his entire being. I can't drag my gaze from his, even as I feel the tension in the room rise around us.

Bowen holds out his hand to me and not for a split-second do I hesitate before placing my palm in his.

An instant later, I am no longer in Harken. Instead, Bowen and I stand in the graveyard beside Sinner's End. Awareness and fear skitter across my exposed skin and I instantly lean closer to him. I remember being here and everything that transpired and it sure as fuck isn't an experience I want to repeat. A shiver works its way through my body, shaking my entire frame before Bowen drapes a fluffy black robe around my shoulders.

"We need to talk," he says gesturing to the cement steps of a crypt. "There are many things I need to explain and this is one of the few places Mana cannot follow and rip you away from me before I get the chance."

I nod, once more placing my hand in his and allowing him to lead me to where he wants. For long moments we sit in silence before he turns to me and speaks.

"Since I can remember, I've watched over you. The moment you took your first breath alongside Emma, I was there to witness it."

"What?" I interrupt, confused.

"Let me finish telling you everything. Then you can ask all the questions your heart desires."

I nod, biting my tongue with effort.

He breathes deeply before continuing. "I watched you your entire life, never once thinking to intervene. But then your parents died and your pain broke my heart. I never made the conscious decision, but a moment later I fell. Not just from Heaven and my Maker, but I fell in love with you."

I gasp, tears steaming down my face as Bowen lays his truth and his heart at my feet.

He smiles sadly. "But I also knew what your life would be like with me. I couldn't protect you from the things in my world if I let you in," he explains. "Not that it matters. You barged in, not leaving me with many options. Now here we are, and I did the only thing I could think of to keep you safe once we all bind ourselves to you. I took power that was never meant for me. I became death itself."

"Fuck..." I mutter lowly.

"That's an apt sentiment," he replies with a chuckle. "I needed to go on a killing spree, murdering in the most violent and vile ways I could ever imagine. And then I had to be killed by some who felt nothing but pure love for me. All the stars had to align perfectly for me to have any chance. Unplanned but ... opportune."

He falls silent, staring at the dirt beneath his feet. I take this as my cue to finally talk.

"What does that mean?" I ask. "Do you need to leave?"

My voice breaks on the last word and Bowen lifts me into his arms, letting me straddle his lap.

"My beautiful girl," he murmurs, rubbing away the tears I didn't know were falling, using the pads of his thumbs. I risked everything—my heart, my soul, my life—to make sure I never had to leave you again. Lethe was created to be by your side for eternity. I was created to watch but never touch or interact. This is me changing my purpose."

"You're staying?"

"If Mana doesn't try to kill me," he says with a chuckle and an eye roll.

"Mana can kiss my ass," I reply angrily. "In this whole mess, no one has ever taken a moment to ask me what I want. Well, except Asmodeus."

"And what did the prince want in return for fulfilling your wishes?"

He looks genuinely curious about what choosing this life cost me.

"I will work for him, doing what Mana does. I will corrupt and reap souls for him until eternity fades away."

"And you're happy with this arrangement?" Bowen asks, a frown creasing his forehead.

"It was the only way. It was my decision to make, just like becoming death was yours."

He nods, smiling as he rubs circles on my back. The silence in the cemetery floods around us like a cloak. It's weird because it feels electric, like a current is running through us over and over. I'm not scared anymore. No, I am excited.

"What now?" I ask, my cheek resting against his chest, his heartbeat silent.

"Whatever you want, Addi. I already gave up everything for you."

"I want you to make love to me," I say softly. "Just you and me, no one else. I want you to be with me and set our bond so no one will ever be able to get between us ever again."

"Addi…"

"No," I cut him off. "This is also my decision. I get to decide who I let into my body and when. And I want you."

Shrugging, I allow the robe he covered me with to fall to the ground, once more exposing my nudity to his gaze. His finger travels along a red line that runs from between my breasts to my pelvic bones, a remnant of Mana's earlier coupling. His violence knew no bounds as he fucked himself into me. Setting our bond for the rest of eternity.

"I love you," Bowen says, drawing me in for a quick kiss. "Let me take you to Harken where I can make love to you in a bed."

"I don't want a bed. I want the real you."

"The real me isn't good enough for you."

"And yet, the real Bowen fell for me, risked his soul for me, protected me, watched over me, gave up everything for me. I think I'm the unworthy one here."

He stares at me in astonishment.

Waving my arm, I gesture at the graveyard. "I was here when you decided to fall, to come to me. Don't you think it's appropriate that you claim me here?"

I watch him as he works through my words. He stands silently, and I wrap my legs around his waist. His erection rubs against my bare, battered pussy with every step we take. He lays me down on a cold slab of cement. It's one of the older graves in the cemetery from when people feared grave robbers. But for us, it is perfect.

Bowen lowers his lips to mine, kisses me gently, languidly before moving on to the rest of my body. He takes his time, paying attention to each breast until my nipples are turgid in the cool air. He skims his lips across my abdomen, tracing the mark that Mana left but is quickly fading away. He kisses each of my hip bones, the insides of my thighs, my calves, and the soles of my feet. It's such a simple thing to do but so revenant it brings tears to my eyes.

I wanted him to show me the real Bowen and that is what he is doing. Behind all the anger, sarcasm, and violence lies a gentle soul. A heart that has claimed my own without even trying.

He kisses his way back up my body, somehow having undressed in the process until he is leaning over me, his hips spreading my legs open, and the head of his cock notched at my entrance.

His onyx wings spread wide before enveloping us as he presses his thick cock into me, inch by torturous inch. My back bows from the cold slab beneath me, my breast pressing against his muscular chest. Bowen strokes into me, slowly but deeper than I ever thought possible. It's overwhelming, angonizingly slow, and utterly perfect.

For long, leisurely moments he makes love to me, his wings protecting us from the elements before his fingers start to strum my clit with a feather-soft precision. Moans and incoherent words fall from my lips as my orgasm crests and breaks, pulling me under. Bowen strains above me, his cock kicking inside me as he floods me with his cum.

Softly, he pushes my hair off my sweat-soaked forehead, nothing but pure, dark obsessive love burning in his darkened gaze.

"You are mine. And I am yours. Not even death can separate us."

Chapter Thirty-Five

The Arms of My Immortal

Kaleb

I turn the glistening flesh of some unidentified meat on the crypt-themed barbecue out the back of Harken for our grand re-opening night, and pray to whatever demon is listening to hear me that it's pork. Or some really big chicken.

The hoards seem to be eating it, and I hope we don't have an impromptu repeat of the succubus night anytime soon because that shit took ages to get out of the damned walls. Walls that still whisper to me no matter which room I try to sleep in.

The drink in my hand has Mana's signature ForgetMeKnot tinge, but his drug is a thing of a bygone era. Harken is clean now.

Well, people still die, but it's by their choice. The *Die For Me* crew sign a liability waiver and head to the lower levels for their fun where Mana and Addi complete their nightly ritual. I still don't know how they're getting the disappearances by the local law and I don't want to know how much it's costing us. Mana claims we're clean and for now, I'm going with that. Blind eye and all. Apparently, love does that, and I love all the creepy fuckers in our strange little pentagonal relationship. Well, almost all.

Bowen sashays by, his arms still wrapped around Addi. The angel-turned-reaper still freaks me out. But our girl has taken to him, and that's all that matters. She nestles into his side like she's meant to be there, dressed in her customary red. Another thing that's stuck after Asmodeus's fateful visit. He's not a lifelong fixture, though apparently, he has his own obsessional problems. Mana refuses to go into it, but the prince of Hell isn't as … clean … as he appears.

Either way, I'm back in leather pants and a vest, though I don't hate them as much as I did back on my first week working Harken behind the bar when I first set eyes on Addi. Hells, that was a long time ago. Or not so long, just … an age.

I snare her slim arm, tugging her easily from Bowen's grip. I offer to trade him for a slab of unidentifiable meat—not my cooking's problem—but he shakes his head. Food doesn't do it for him anymore.

He looks a little bereft without her in his arms, standing off from the crowd who give the void of his space a wide berth. It took us a good few days to realize no one else can see him.

Or, more to the point, they can't see him until he needs them to see him, usually as he escorts them to where the hell ever souls go *after*, when they aren't being locked up in Harken's stones, awaiting collection by Mana's hellish father.

The politics of the underworld blow my mind. Apparently, none of us have to worry about that for an eternity, and there's enough right here to keep me occupied.

"Enjoying the party, Addi?" I trail my fingers along her velvet halter neck top, sliding them into the valley between her breasts to play with her in plain sight.

Addi writhes in my arms, gasping a little. A telltale flush stains her cheeks. I can't work out if it's arousal, embarrassment, or a bit of both. Our level of possession with our once-human goes well beyond the bounds of any sense of normality. We're all still getting used to that, Addi most of all. She signed up for the same eternity as us, she just didn't seem to think about what that quite meant.

"Kaleb," she mewls as my fingers latch onto her nipple, milking her gently one-handed as I flip barbeque with the other.

"Mmm, kitten?" My voice rasps, my cock hardening as I think about abandoning my cooking duties to flip her over the nearest faux crypt stone and sink balls-deep into her pretty, well cunt. "Something you need?"

Her bare legs press to my thigh, and I give her all the encouragement she needs to mount me, pushing my knee between hers. Mana came in hard and fast with a *dress and no panties* rule for ease of access the moment she complained about us ruining her favorite clothing. It's been a boon to us and a deficit to her but our girl is always ready, always wet, no matter how much she complains.

"Kaleb..." Her voice trails off, filled with a pending whine.

I fix her with a hard stare. "You want to get off, kitten? I want your scent all over me. Rub." Rolling her nipple just so, I tease her right to the edge, knowing how much she loved nipple play. Two would get her off given enough time. One? It's not quite what she needs, and right now that's perfect.

"But, the people—" she stammers, her gaze flitting side to side.

I hold her pretty eyes for a long moment, and nod. Giving her an inch of reprieve, I jerk my chin up. "All right. Here's a little cover for you. But I want a nice display and a long, wet mark on my thigh where you've creamed all over me, understand?" My voice turns harsh with need.

What started as a fun tease devolves into something darker within seconds, as usual.

Lethe's long-fingered hands rest on her slim waist as he presses against her back, and waits. His pupils are blown wide with arousal already. My little submissive angel is always on edge, but he's trained well, and he won't act without mine or Mana's direct command.

I give him a single shake of my head. This is Addi's task. He's just there to provide cover, and to watch her. It's enough as he sucks in every part of her. Bowen drifts over to watch, providing an extra dynamic Addi can't follow, too lost in her arousal, but I see it. Bowen almost isn't aware of the effect he has on our resident fallen, but Lethe stiffens visibly at the reaper's proximity. He trails a finger along her side, her flesh wavering as she whimpers at his occasionally acidic touch.

"Pretty," he murmurs, the faintest scent of sulphur mingling with hers.

Lethe looks green, but after all this time I'm getting used to it. Concealing a smirk, I pinch Adreana's nipple harder until she's biting her lips hard to conceal the pain. Her breaths come fast as Lethe pushes into her from behind, Bowen crowding her side. She looks around wildly but again I shake my head.

"Your attention is here, Addi," I murmur, tapping the tip of her imprisoned nipple. "Come for me. Or..." I tap the prongs I've left on the grill, where they sit in the heat.

Fear turns her eyes white and hells, is it a beautiful sight.

"You wouldn't—" she chokes, her eyes locked on the heated torture tool I threaten her with. Not that I'd do it, but...

"*I will.*" Mana liberates the tongs from my hand.

"Kaleb gave you an order. Now, Adreana." His voice is fathomless, a wicked siren call none of us can escape.

She claws at me, arching as I return to milking her, easing off the pain. Her pretty pussy rubs my thigh, smearing her cream over me as requested, but it's not enough.

"Come for us," I murmur, leaning in to steal a kiss. Simple, but the moment I slide my tongue into her mouth I realize my mistake.

Hot and wet, all I want is to plunge myself deep into her pussy. Hands reach around me, freeing my cock, working me as I tease her. I grunt into her mouth as she rubs herself into a frenzy, coming for me exactly as I demanded.

But she's not alone.

Her sweet mouth has always been my kryptonite. It's like tonguing her wet pussy, plunging my cock into her depths. The cool hand that works me belongs to the master we all serve. Just as she stares up at me, my name on her lips as she trembles on my thigh, heat gushing between her legs to coat me, Mana whispers something in hellspeak, a name, perhaps. I explode all over his hand and the front of her red dress, staining her white.

"Fuck," I mumble into her mouth, sagging back into him.

Addi comes too, still wrapped around the thigh I press between her legs. The fallen watches us both with hungry eyes. If I ordered him on clean-up duty, he'd find the sin-soaked ground with his knees right now. Bowen watches us all with a small smile.

But right now isn't for them. At least, not yet. Maybe that can come after.

I turn my head back, letting Mana find my mouth with his in a long, deep kiss of mingled need and gratitude.

"Christ, hellspawn," he murmurs against my mouth. "That was meant to be for her."

"Try not to be trouble for the rest of the night." I raise a hand despite my instant exhaustion and slap his cheek firmly.

The demon's eyes glow as I turn back to Addi, tucking her breast back into her dress and seek her mouth for a slow, long kiss. A different pair of hands fixes the front of my pants while Mana turns back to the barbeque I abandoned. With a few flicks of his long fingers, Lethe has me ready to go again. I give his wrist a firm squeeze with dual purpose—a thank you for his service and a warning not to overstep. The corners of his lips flicker, and I wonder that we haven't raised ourselves a prime brat in the making.

Addi slips into the space between my arms, resting her head on my chest. "Help me change?" she asks, looking up at me with sleepy eyes.

I stare down at her, a dark laugh ripping from my chest. "Hell no, kitten. We both wear each other's marks tonight for everyone to see."

Her cheeks flame as red as her dress. She nods, biting her lips though I know underneath the added humiliation she's pleased. Addi never says no to a display of ownership, especially not when it involves us wearing hers. Turnabout is only fair after all, and I'm far from embarrassed to have her claim us, me, in every way possible.

A single nod and she's on her toes, pressing her mouth against my lips in a fierce, possessive kiss of her own. Her hands find Mana's behind me. The demon twitches against my back, as pleased with her after display as me.

Not to be forgotten, she reaches blindly for Bowen and Lethe who wrap themselves around her, their ongoing feud forgotten in lieu of their overwhelming love for her.

The human who brought four fallen, unforgiven creatures together. It's the sort of fairy story no child should ever be told, but that's not the aim of stories told in the dark, quiet hours after midnight.

I trail my fingers through her hair. "Love you," I murmur lazily, as though hundreds of people aren't waiting for their food while Mana cremates the lot.

They can wait. Besides, Harken's entry clause does have some obscure wording about those lower levels. A "just in case" liability option to cover my girl's peachy ass and ours in case she or our resident reaper needs to go on the rampage.

Turns out our little bratty fallen has an eye for contract law. Who knew.

She tilts her head to one side, her eyes aglow with the sort of fervor that promises a damn fine night in the making.

"Mine." Her gaze sweeps across every male she claims, marking us.

"All of you."

The girl we unite for, push away enmity and feuds that would otherwise end us all.

Ours for an eternity.

JADE MARSHALL AND RAVEN HUSH

Epilogue
The God Complex

Asmodeus

"You understand the terms?"

I watch the young woman who sits across the oak desk from me with narrowed eyes. All faded blonde streaks grown out to her dark roots and sallow skin that hangs below eyes that once sparkled now are dull. This creature is lost. There is no better place for her than Hell's Gate. But she must prove to me that she needs my help before I allow her into my institute.

"I read the contract." A faint degree of her previous bratty behavior ekes through her exhausted facade.

Except, her fatigue is real. She's hit her limit. This is what's left at the end of a long run of endless parties, greed, and drugs of a very specific variety.

I nod slowly, accepting that she needs the help only I can provide. "And you agree to the treatment? Once you're in my care there is no simply walking away," I caution.

My guest picks at lint baubled on her pink jumpsuit that fits to her lightly curved frame, so similar to her twin sister's. "I understand. I can't keep going," she whispers.

A breath escapes me as my lips purse. "The program is arduous. It isn't kind. I'll need you to sign every page. Please take your time and read through each," I say kindly, knowing she won't.

Emma flips her hair back, but her dirty locks fall over her face as she leans forward and signs her freedom over to me with a shaking hand. Her brow creases as she reaches the last page. It's always the hardest.

I place my hand lightly over hers. "It's all right. I understand."

Thick lashes flutter as she looks through them at me. "I don't want to be alone anymore. Promise me?" A single tear falls.

In a previous life she might have used that move to intimidate or manipulate. Today she bares all in the most honest sign of trust I believe she's ever given anyone.

I squeeze her fingers and lie to her face. "I promise. You'll never be alone again."

The corners of her mouth strain but she can't smile. It will be a long time before that happens for her, if she ever can again in my care. Without reading the final clause on my contract, she signs her name, sliding her fingertips along the sheaf and tidying the pile as she hands them back.

A gasp escapes her lips as the sharp edges of the pure white paper designed to do exactly that slices her flesh open in the slightest of papercuts. Just enough to leave her mark on the page.

She stares at the bloodstain as more tears fall. "I'm sorry."

"It's fine, Emma. Welcome to Heaven's Gate Rehabilitation Center." I place the papers in the top drawer of my desk, shut and lock it, pocketing the key in plain sight.

Her eyes track the movement, an action designed to instil doubt on an already teetering subject. My program has begun.

"Maybe I—" she begins.

I cut her off. "Shall I show you to your room?" It's not a question.

Emma nods, resigned, and lets me take her bag from her limp fingers. The moment her body is close to mine I feel it. Fainter than with her sister, but the same sense of possession. She is not Adreana, but she'll do nicely to fill the spot my spawn stole from me.

She stops, her head tilted to one side and when she looks up at me, some of the old Emma is there, a spark of sexual awakening. No, that part of her isn't dead, just worn through. Empty. That's all right, we can top that up together. We have all the time in eternity, after all. Hours and days don't matter at Heaven's Gate.

She really should have read the terms more closely.

Her heart-shaped face tips back, her body so tiny I could place my hands around her waist and squeeze my fingers together easily on either side to touch them again, dwarfing her. Overpower her with nothing but literal size. Some part of me likes that imagery, and I file it away to play with later.

Her fingers raise to stroke the front of my pristine white shirt beneath the white overcoat. A professional-looking touch I like when I'm in this form. Her contact isn't the usual for this situation, but her interest amuses me, and I allow it for now. An experiment conducted under controlled circumstances.

"You ... you remind me of someone," she whispers.

I match her faint smile. "It's the eyes," I whisper back, blinking slowly, allowing my irises to darken for an instant, letting her glimpse the similarities.

"Mana?" Her murmur, filled with all the hate, the confusion, the sexual longing of their past iteration hits me like a drug of its own.

Yes, Emma will be fun to play with during her stay.

"My son and I share many … similarities."

I let that thought swim in the charged air between us. Picking a memory out of her thoughts, I trail my fingertips across her nape like he did right before he pushed her to her knees and filled her mouth with his thick cock once.

Not that she remembers the incident actively, due to the unusual qualities of his bodily secretions. Mine have other properties.

"Oh." Her sigh lights my blood in a way I haven't felt in an eon.

I continue walking, carrying her bag in a death grip that nearly tears the handle from the item with the need flowing through me. Control is the ultimate test, it won't do to ruin her before I've had time torturing my new plaything.

"I believe you'll find the facilities … hygienic."

It's not the word any of my wards expect, and I try to always keep them off balance. They're more manageable and far more fun that way.

"All right." Fresh uncertainty fills her voice.

"This is where you will eat." I point out the empty cafeteria, with its bare row of never used bain-maries, and the spotless dining hall.

"That looks welcoming." Her voice lilts before a small, dry cough evicts from her throat. "I'm thirsty. Is there something…?"

"It's the air. It irritates everyone. Something to do with the evaporator." I'm getting my quota of fibs in early today. "This way."

I lead her along a bright white corridor that matches the entire decor of Heaven's Gate, my footsteps absent in this place along with my shadow and hers, but she's too overwhelmed to notice. White walls are the standard that seem to glow from within. This matches the floors, the ceilings, and as such there is no need for windows or lighting. My institution is completely blocked off from the outside world. From reality in every sense.

Once a patient walks in those doors, they will never leave, ever again. Not feel sunlight on their skin, not taste fresh air, or rain on their lips.

Nor will they be able to die.

She really should have read the terms before she signed.

I sigh my contentment as we pass closed doors. Twenty-two rooms, all white, all the same. Some are empty, while others are filled. Emma will bring our current total complement up to fifty percent capacity.

In the center of the corridor, I place her bag on the floor beside her door and swipe a card to the reader beside it. The lock clicks open to expose a stark, white room filled with basic furniture. Every piece, including the bed, has curved edges only. It won't do to allow my patients to hurt themselves on sharp things whilst in my care.

No blankets, no sheets, no cushions. No carpet. Nothing, except for what she brings with her. A gesture of hope I allow for a while longer.

"Welcome," I murmur, gesturing her inside the room.

Emma dithers at the threshold. This is my least favorite part. The need to push her inside strengthens with each breath, but I can't make this decision for her. Signature or not, she must cross into the room of her own free will.

"When does the treatment start?" she whispers, staring through the doorway that glows at the edges.

The room itself has a radiance to it, though she won't realize that never goes away until she tries to sleep, and can't. That's step one, and my program is endless.

"We have started, Emma," I prompt her gently. "Please enter the room. I'll be with you in a moment." Ever in character, I smile kindly and dip a shoulder forward as if to touch her, crowding her space.

She shivers, and takes that singular step I so desperately need.

The door slides shut, her sectioned out on one side, me on the other with her things. Her eyes widen as she realizes the door is slightly opaque, that she can't reach me though she can still see me.

First comes the confusion, then the begging eyes. After that, anger. It's a beautiful cycle, and I wish I could relive this first time forever with her.

Perfection.

All too soon it's over. Still, the pure panic on her features leaves me hard and aching. Her cry, soundless on my side of the silent, white corridor, is a beautiful thing. Tears well as she pounds the door uselessly, the last remnants of her rage turning her face darker than her jumpsuit. Soon that will be stripped from her too, and she'll wear a uniform of my choosing.

I smile at her gently through the door as her image fades, the door closing out our vision of each other until I stand in a hallway of pure white silence.

Smiling faintly, I walk back to my office and sit with her bag beside my desk, unopened. She won't be needing it, and I'll throw it into a trash can the next time I visit my son in his hideous realm.

Until then, I hum softly to myself and plan all the ways I will enjoy breaking my brand-new toy.

And how much fun I'll have introducing her to my other pets.

The End

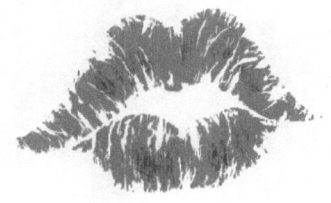

EVERNIGHT PUBLISHING ®

www.evernightpublishing.com

www.ingramcontent.com/pod-product-compliance
Lightning Source LLC
Chambersburg PA
CBHW050722180626
46814CB00002B/555